Y0-ARD-935

MAR - - 2022

SPECIAL MESSAGE TO READERS
THE ULVERSCROFT FOUNDATION
(registered UK charity number 264873)
was established in 1972 to provide funds for
research, diagnosis and treatment of eye diseases.
Examples of major projects funded by the
Ulverscroft Foundation are:-

- The Children's Eye Unit at Moorfelds Eye Hospital, London
- The Ulverscroft Children's Eye Unit at Great Ormond Street Hospital for Sick Children
- Funding research into eye diseases and treatment at the Department of Ophthalmology, University of Leicester
- The Ulverscroft Vision Research Group, Institute of Child Health
- Twin operating theatres at the Western Ophthalmic Hospital, London
- The Chair of Ophthalmology at the Royal Australian College of Ophthalmologists

You can help further the work of the Foundation
by making a donation or leaving a legacy. Every
contribution is gratefully received. If you would
like to help support the Foundation or require
further information, please contact:

THE ULVERSCROFT FOUNDATION
The Green, Bradgate Road, Anstey
Leicester LE7 7FU, England
Tel: (0116) 236 4325
website: www.ulverscroft-foundation.org.uk

SHADOW VALLEY RISING

Ella Mae Campbell traveled west with her family in a wagon train in 1860. But she never made it to Denver City with them. During a terrifying attack, she was taken captive by marauding Indians. No one thought she would survive — or would even want to after her ordeal. But survive she did. Yet after she was rescued, she — like so many other captives — found herself shunned by the very settlers who'd organized the search party for her . . .

STEPHEN OVERHOLSER

♦

SHADOW VALLEY RISING

Complete and Unabridged

LINFORD
Leicester

First published in the United States
by Five Star

First Linford Edition
published 2022
by arrangement with
Golden West Literary Agency

Copyright © 2002 by Stephen Overholser
All rights reserved

*A catalogue record for this book is available
from the British Library.*

ISBN 978–1–78541–969–0

Published by
Ulverscroft Limited
Anstey, Leicestershire

Printed and bound in Great Britain by
TJ Books Ltd., Padstow, Cornwall

This book is printed on acid-free paper

Prologue

With each bite of a mason's chisel, one-hundred-year-old mortar chipped and crumbled under sledge-hammer blows, disintegrating into a fine, gray powder. The stonemason, a member of this First Brethren Church in Denver, Colorado, had volunteered his services. The work went quickly, and the granite cornerstone was soon loosened by pry bars.

With shoulders hunched, onlookers were bundled against a north wind bearing snowflakes. They watched as two more volunteers looped a strap behind the block. The strap was secured to a rented backhoe. Diesel engine roaring, the arm of the shovel seemed to flex with a steel muscle. The granite block slid out slowly, with a dull grinding sound of stone on stone. It came free in a small shower of powdered mortar. The operator shut off the engine. A moment of awed silence held the onlookers before Pastor Sue Tracy stepped forward.

As planned by the congregation, she would be the first person in a century to see the contents. Church records had been lost in the 1965 flood of the South Platte River, and until this moment no one gathered here knew what the cavity in the cornerstone contained — if anything.

Video and still cameras recorded Pastor Tracy's movements as she leaned over the stone block. She peered into the opening. Then she reached in. She drew out a rectangular, shoebox-size bundle wrapped in brown oilcloth. Turning, she held it up for all to see. After a scattering of applause, the congregation filed into the sanctuary. They shed their coats and hats and sat in the pews, leaning forward in quiet anticipation. All eyes were on the pastor when she set the bundle on an old, heavy-legged table that had been placed in front of the pulpit for the day's ceremony.

The oilcloth broke at every fold, coming to pieces as she opened it. She uncovered a steel strongbox with

Colorado Fuel & Iron stamped into the lid. The latch and two hinges of brass were barely tarnished. Sue Tracy pressed the latch and raised the lid. On top was a rolled sheepskin. She lifted it out and unrolled it, holding it up for all to see. The document was decorated with a flowery border and inscribed in the bold, elaborate lettering reminiscent of a property deed or stock certificate of the era.

She smoothed it out, and gave strong voice to the message crossing a century:

**Eighteen Hundred and
Ninety-Nine
This 31st day of December,
the congregation of the First
Brethren Church
conveys heart-felt greetings to
you on the last day of the century.**

**Borne on invisible wings of faith
from our congregation to yours,
from our century to yours,
we place herein a cross and Bible,**

penned messages from our
congregation,
and the diaries of Ella Mae
Campbell,
'A woman of noble character and
virtue.' (Proverbs 31:10)

We mortals know the Past.
The Present we see around us.
The Future is held in the hands
of God.

Brethren in our sacred
fellowship,
as we ponder lives yet to be,
we modestly describe ours,
to share steadfast faith in
God Almighty.

4

Part One

Part One

1

In the moments of complete darkness before the prairie dawn, Ella Mae opened her eyes. She lifted her head, and then came up on her elbows, peering into the night. Something had awakened her — probably a raccoon or porcupine lumbering past her bedding under the Campbell wagon.

Darkness. Her quilt slipped from her shoulders when she sat up. A deep chill coursed through her as she realized what was wrong. The fire was out.

Every night since the wagons had been ferried across the Mississippi River at St. Joseph, Missouri, wood had been burned within the circle of wagons. On the advice of the wagon master, Buell Harris, a small fire was kept alive through the night, the flames serving as a message to savages that the men and women

7

of this wagon train could not be taken by surprise. One at a time, armed settler men stood shifts of four hours, each one feeding the fire while guarding livestock confined within the circle of Conestoga wagons and freight outfits.

Now Ella yearned to cry out, but could not draw a breath. Dark figures were out there, men moving swiftly, shadow-silent. In the next instant a shot from a musket brought the camp to life.

'Savages! Savages!'

A man's panicked shout stirred other voices, shrieks and yells in sudden confusion. Gunshots boomed. Ella saw flames darting from musket barrels like the red tongues of snakes. Amid shouts came shrill war whoops. Then a torch sputtered and flared into flames.

Firebrands from last night's cook fires touched the wicks of lanterns, and by their wavering light, Ella saw naked men among milling horses and mules and oxen. On the far side of the camp a big freight wagon eased out of its place in the circle, rolling back slowly like a ship drifting from its moorings.

Savages shouted in high-pitched calls while herding horses to the opening left by the freight wagon. Balls whined through the air as more guns were discharged. Ella turned toward a cry of pain from the Osborne wagon. In the next instant she heard thumps in the wagon box overhead. The tailgate dropped.

By the glow of torches and lanterns she saw her father leap out, long-barreled musket in hand. Clad only in long underwear, he sprinted into the circle. Ella realized her mouth had stretched open and her lungs burned in an involuntary cry, a plea to bring her father back, to stop him from running to his death.

Fiery torches seemed to dance through her nightmare. She heard men's voices, all of them strained and cursing as though demanding order from chaos. One stout settler, his baggy trousers held up a single suspender slanting across his bare chest, met and struggled with a dim figure that had leaped out of the space between two wagons.

Ella recognized the settler, a stout, full-bearded German named Ludwig Gustafson who spoke no English, and then she saw the glint of a knife in a thrusting hand. The big man grew still, not moving until he sank to his knees and toppled over. A naked warrior, cast in wavering light, let out a yelping cry.

'Ella Mae! Ella Mae!'

Her name shouted by her mother seemed to be part of a mad dream. She heard the familiar voice, at once sobbing and summoning, pleading with her to get into the wagon. Ella kicked the quilt away. She scurried back, crab-like, her instincts demanding escape from the mighty struggles of men killing and being killed. She rose up. The moment she straightened, she was grabbed from behind.

Bare arms encircled her chest, tightening until her breasts hurt. She was lifted off her feet. She kicked and fought. Her mind raging, her voice silenced, she was carried into darkness while her mother called her name.

Ella writhed, struggling against the iron grasp of a man who reeked of sweat and smoke. She twisted her head around and tried to bite into flesh, but could not reach him. She bounced with his jogging stride while he fled into darkness. Sporadic musket-fire and hoarse shouts faded in the distance.

* * *

Girls dragged from their beds by blood-drinking savages were only scare stories whispered in the safety of a bedroom, curtains drawn, coal stove creaking. At home, when her imagination had soared into nightmares, Ella was always rescued by her father's calming voice or the soft stroke of her mother's hand. But now, when she opened her eyes, she saw a dim glow over a horizon as flat as an ironing board. This day had dawned, and the nightmare lived.

She was carried through clumps of sagebrush and pear cactus. Shards of

11

sandstone stood on end here, placed randomly by the ancient forces of nature. Her captor ran awkwardly past jutting rocks that might have marked graves in a bizarre prairie cemetery. Ella glimpsed a long shadow ahead — a crease in the terrain. Her captor ran to it, leaped into a dry ravine, and dropped her.

Ella landed hard in warm sand. With the air knocked out of her, she could not inhale for a long moment. She thought she would die. Then she gasped, breathing raggedly to fill her lungs. She sensed a man's presence and looked up.

Silhouetted against the pale sky, her captor stood over her. The broad face of the man was scored by a web of black lines and a thick band of white paint under each eye. Two braids of black hair fell to his shoulders. Nude but for a breechcloth and moccasins, he leaned down, reaching out to touch her skin.

By instinct, Ella pulled her legs together. Summoning strength unknown to her, she pushed his probing hands away. In a flash of impatience, he grasped the front of her nightdress and ripped it open from neckline to hem.

Ella's fingers curled into claws. Fight or die was the sole thought in her mind as she stared up at the warrior's impassive face. Then a war cry reached them, and he turned away. Ella gathered fabric around her and watched him rush to a cluster of spotted ponies in the ravine. The animals pranced when the warrior grabbed a rope strung through horsehair bridles. He held the rope taut to control the animals, and turned toward the bank of the ravine — watching, waiting.

Ella stood. The warrior's attention was no longer on her. She backed away, one slow step at a time. Then she spun around, dug her toes into the sand, and sprinted down the ravine with the torn nightdress billowing open.

The ravine deepened. Ella glanced back. She was not followed. Hope welling within her, she made a quick decision. Angling to the bank on her right, she leaped and tried to get a foothold that would propel her upward and out of the ravine. Soft soil gave way, cascading downward in a small avalanche. Falling back, she slid to the bottom, gasping.

She looked back. The warrior held the spotted ponies, still staring at the crest of the ravine. He had not seen her, or, if he had, he was occupied with a task that was more important to him.

Ella looked up again, now seeing a clump of gray sagebrush. Gathering fuel for fires on this prairie had taught her that desert sage was deeply rooted. If she could reach that gnarled trunk no thicker than her wrist, she could pull herself out of this ravine. At once she knew it was too far away and too high for her to reach in a single leap. Yet it was her only hope.

Ella backed away six paces. Bent at the waist with legs flexed, she measured the distance. *Impossible . . . too far away . . . .* She pushed doubts from her mind, drew a deep breath, and ran. At the bank she leaped, thrusting a hand upward.

She missed the trunk, but grasped a small branch. The branch bent with her weight, but did not snap off. Holding on, she frantically reached up with her other hand, grabbed the sagebrush, and dug her toes into soft soil. The power of her churning legs thrust her upward, promising escape until a pair of hands encircled her waist.

She was yanked downward. Her captor flung her to the ground. Consciousness nearly left her as darkness closed in and sounds faded. She was aware of hands grasping her ankles. Dragged back toward the ponies, pain shot through her side. Dream-like, she realized she had been kicked by a moccasined foot.

She doubled up. Her captor kicked her again. Alert now, Ella did not cry out. For a reason she could not fathom, she was determined to hide her pain, to deny him the satisfaction of knowing he had hurt her.

As a last warning, the painted warrior cuffed her before returning to the ponies. Her cheek stinging, Ella knew he was crudely dominating her, teaching her obedience under threat of pain, or worse.

She heard a distant sound — hoof beats growing louder. Sitting up, she brushed strands of hair from her eyes. She stared at the man's muscular back as he held the horses.

I will never obey you. She tried to shout her defiance, but no sounds came from her mouth. She turned her head toward the rumblings, listening to the hoof beats with the growing awareness that those rhythmic sounds matched the pounding of her heart. In the next instant, horses spilled over the brink of the ravine, lunging and plunging to the bottom.

Driven by the shrill whistles of their captors, two dozen saddle mounts made a great, rolling wave. At the bottom they wheeled and fled, or tried to. Warriors raised their arms and waved them back. The horses reared and milled, eyes rolling. Ella saw warriors leap onto the backs of their ponies. They rode away from her, driving the stolen horses to the shallow end of the ravine.

Huddled against the bank, she shielded her face from air filled with dust and grit.

The raiders had completed their theft swiftly, without a word between them, and through it all she had been ignored. She stood, new hope surging through her. She backed away, and halted, aware of a man's presence before she saw him.

Like a shadow within a shadow, a lone rider emerged from the cloud of dust stirred by horses. The pale light of morning shone on two white slashes under the dark eyes. A web of lines lent ferocity to his gaze. Her captor rode to her, leaned down, and gathered her up in one outstretched arm. He ignored her clawing hands and kicking feet, and pulled her over the pony's back.

Ella first tried to bite him, then scratched at his bare thigh. He struck her as the pony climbed out of the ravine.

Looking back, Ella saw a world turned upside down. A haze of smoke marked the circle of wagons and half a dozen freight outfits. Canvas wagon covers, once as white as sails, were now weathered to a color remarkably similar to the lifeless gray-brown of this barren land.

17

The pony's gait jarred her view, but she made out four men, all of them running toward the ravine. One gestured frantically.

Father!

Tears blurred her gaze. In the distance Earl Campbell halted. He dropped to one knee. Elbow resting on his other knee, he steadied the heavy musket and drew aim. Smoke plumed from the barrel.

Delayed by distance, the report reached her. The other men halted, aimed, and fired. They reloaded, plunged ramrods into barrels, cocked hammers, and fired again. From this distance the shots seemed harmless until a musket ball whistled past her captor. The warrior ducked, and gave his pony a kick.

Ella wished one of the bullets would knock him off his pony. Failing that, she wished the bullet would strike her, ending this nightmare. In the next instant the spotted pony topped a rise and plunged down the far side, cutting off her view of the circled wagons.

2

'Horse!'

Earl Campbell shouted for help as he ran back to the wagons, his face glistening with sweat, chest heaving. He was followed by the three men he had led in a mad foot-chase after the raiders.

'I . . . need . . . I need a . . . horse!'

Not until he had heard his wife's anguished cries at the break of dawn had he learned of the tragedy — savages had taken their daughter.

Earl Campbell had run after them. Three bachelors traveling with the party had joined the chase, muskets loaded and cocked. But when Earl saw the war party, mounted and driving horses out of a ravine at full gallop, he knew he could not catch them on foot. Halting, he had fired until the savages were out of range. Then he had run back to camp.

'Horse!'

His plea went unanswered. Men,

women, and children wandered about in their nightclothes, empty-eyed, dazed. A few tended the wounded — settler men lying on the ground where they had fallen. Tomahawked and knifed in the mêlée, Buell Harris and the German settler, Gustafson, were among the dead. So was Clara Osborne.

Mourned by her husband and five young children, her body lay in a pool of darkening blood in their wagon. She had been shot through the neck by a musket ball while she had huddled there with her children. Now the children clutched their father, a taciturn man sobbing with a child's abandon.

'Give me the loan of a saddle horse!'

Sweat beaded Earl's brow and dripped from the end of his nose. He was a man in a rage, glowering at the people who had become his friends in the eight weeks since the Brethren Wagon Company was formed in St. Joe, Missouri.

Finally a deep-voiced man answered: 'Sir, I have lost every Morgan horse I own. Prime breeding stock all the way from Richmond, sir. Stolen. Gone for good.'

Earl wheeled to face Levi Case. Flanked by his two teen-aged sons, Case was a barrel-chested man with a long beard streaked with silver, white hair combed straight back from a high forehead. He was a gentleman who addressed all grown men as 'sir' and women as 'ma'am.' He never spoke of his past, but was said to be a grieving widower who was seeking a new life on the frontier.

'To hell with your horses! Don't you know what's happened?'

Earl's shouted question brought silence, not action. Millicent Campbell came running to her husband, a slender woman covered by her nightdress and a shawl thrown over her shoulders. She embraced him, but he pulled away. Thrusting his musket into the air, he cocked the weapon and pulled the trigger.

The loud *boom* startled everyone. Children shrieked and began crying again. Settlers drew back from Earl as

21

though facing a man gone mad. Case's sons, Jared and Jason, eyed him. Jared, the older at sixteen, reached for a holstered pistol.

'Give me a horse!' Earl repeated. 'Give me a horse, and I will chase down those savages . . . .'

Millicent cried out: 'My God! They took our girl. Don't you care? The savages . . . they . . . took her!' Her narrow shoulders quaked as she sobbed; her shouted words only confirming a truth too awful to bear.

'Where is Mister Harris?' Earl demanded.

Levi Case turned. He pointed to a brown woolen blanket on the ground near a covered wagon. 'Sir, our beloved wagon master lies there. So does Mister Hayes, the gentleman on watch last night. Both slain by savages.'

Earl stared at the blanket covering the two men, his disbelief choked by anger. He knew Roger Hayes to be a good man. And Buell Harris had been a commanding figure, trail-wise and even-handed, since the day on the bank of the Mississippi when he had been hired by the men of the Brethren Wagon Company. If he were alive now, orders would be issued and swiftly obeyed. Men would be organized into a search party, armed and mounted, ready to ride.

'Earl, the horses that warn't stoled, why, they's spread out all over hell-an'-gone. It's gonna take time to git a-holt of them.'

Earl faced Henry Rheims, one of the bachelors who had joined him in the abbreviated chase. Likeable, with a quick grin, the young man leaned against his musket, dour now, as he spoke in a low voice. He was one of a dozen bachelors traveling with the wagon company, young men seeking riches in the storied gold fields of Colorado Territory.

'Time!' Earl shouted. 'I don't have time! Every minute takes her farther away.'

'Cleeve's always braggin' up his mules,' Rheims said. 'Says they's broke to saddle. Says a jack can outlast a horse any day of the week.'

In long strides, Earl rushed to a freight wagon near the opening in the circle. Bernard Cleeve owned three large vehicles. Wagon boxes were packed with goods ranging from hardware, boots, clothing, and notions to the tempered steel plow blades and barrels of grain lashed to the sideboards. One of his wagons had been rolled out of place by the savages.

'Cleeve!' Earl shouted. 'Cleeve!'

A balding, black-bearded man stuck his head out of the back of a freight wagon. 'I hear you, Earl, I hear. Get yourself a saddle. Take one of my critters. Luck to you.'

Cleeve spoke through a clenched jaw. He had been relieved to discover the raiders had passed over mules and oxen. Tribesmen roaming this great plain were superb horsemen. Either they did not know what to make of the long-eared, snorting mules, or simply wanted no part of the strange beasts on general principles.

Either way, loaning a mule clearly

ran against Cleeve's better judgment. Without his draft animals, his fortune in merchandise was lost. He had no real choice, though, with Earl glowering at him, the man undoubtedly willing to take a mule with or without permission.

The loan of one mule increased by four when other men volunteered to ride with Earl Campbell. Rheims was the first. Two more bachelors, Daniel Moore and Luther Smith, had lost their horses in the raid, and came to Earl's side, guns in hand, carrying their saddles, blankets, and bridles. The fourth was an older man, Peter Howell. He brought borrowed gear.

'No,' Earl said when he saw that his friend had dressed and buckled a cartridge belt with a holstered revolver around his waist. 'Peter, no.'

Howell shook his head with a faint smile. A minister of the First Brethren Church, he had answered the call to leave home and hearth to bring the Holy Word to immigrants. Now his gray-eyed expression was resolute as he met

Earl's gaze.

'You cannot stop me, Earl.'

The Campbells and Howells, two couples in their early forties, had been close since the day of their departure. Both men were too old for this strenuous trek across half a continent. Both had an only daughter, girls within six months of one another. Other families were larger, the parents younger. The Campbells and the Howells had shared cook fires and daily chores ever since.

'This is my fight,' Earl said. He turned his back to his wife who had been joined by Jane Howell. The two women embraced, with the Howell's daughter, Christina, standing nearby in night-clothes, distraught.

Campbell lowered his voice. 'If I don't make it back, Peter, I want you to look out for Millie . . . .'

Howell shook his head again. 'I will ride with you or behind you. Short of hog-tying me, you cannot stop me.'

'Then I *will* tie you down . . . .'

'Not without a fight,' Howell interrupted, smiling.

Earl stared at him. Neither physically strong nor well armed, Peter Howell was ill-suited for a hard ride to hunt down savages. Earl knew that. Yet, without hesitation, this friend of eight weeks was prepared to risk his life for Ella Mae.

Earl's jaw tightened to hold back his emotions. Clearly there would be no arguing with the man, even if there had been time for debate.

* * *

Ella opened her eyes when the pony halted. She had closed her eyes during the jarring ride, as though somehow she could shut out reality. She had failed, and, when her captor abruptly shoved her off the pony, she staggered and fell, scraping her knees raw. She drew a breath and winced, ribs hurting.

Aware of men's eyes on her, Ella gathered the nightdress around her, covering herself as best she could. She looked around. The surrounding terrain was

27

unlike the short-grass prairie marked by sage and pear cactus. Here, the vast land was not scored by the twin ruts of wagon wheels, a trail leading caravans to the setting sun. The raiding party was surrounded by sand hills, rounded mounds standing barren but for thin tufts of grass. Hot, deathly silent, and bone dry, somehow this empty land brought to mind the cresting waves of a high sea.

Sea. The sound of splashing water drew her attention to the bronzed men squatting around a cluster of white rocks. A spring pooled at their feet. Stirred water sparkled like the diamonds of a queen's crown. Parched mouth open, Ella got to her feet. She made her way toward the spring. The warriors ignored her until she drew near. One spoke. Her captor quickly looked around, saw her, and reached down for a stone at his feet. He pitched it at her, hard.

The rock struck her cheek an inch below her eye. She cried out, more in rage than pain. She touched the wound and looked at her fingertips. They were bloody. The wound was not deep, but the indignity of it filled her with a rage she had never known before. She wanted to shriek at that man, at all of them, somehow to defeat them. Anger cut off her voice. She turned away. Tears seemed to burst from deep within, as though a dam had suddenly given way.

Since dawn her mind had only coped with the immediate, but now fragmented memories crept into her thoughts. Images of her mother and father reeled through her mind, along with the Howells and their daughter, Christina, who had become her best friend. Memories swelled her emotions like water seeping into a sponge. In those moments the past loomed larger than the present, as though she had retreated from this horror. Walking beside her family's wagon mile after mile, the hated daily chores, the endless dust churned by hoofs and wheels — all of those memories were vivid. Her captivity by savages could not be real.

She pressed roughened hands to her

eyes, drew a deep breath, and stopped the sobs. Touching her face again, she felt a knot below her eye where the stone had hit her. It was sore and oozed blood.

A whistled call, repeated and then answered, made her turn and follow the gazes of the warriors. Their attention was fixed on the crest of a sandy hill a hundred yards distant. A lone horseman topped that rounded hilltop. He came toward them, slowly, riding with caution born of survival in a hostile land.

Ella watched this man riding bareback on a black pony with patches of white and a blaze face. Bare-chested, he was not painted like the others. He wore fringed leggings of tanned leather and a single feather in his braided hair. He carried a bow. A quiver of arrows was slung over his back.

He came to the spring and gracefully slid off his pony. Greeted by the warriors, he acknowledged them one by one. A head taller than the others, he pointed to the stolen horses and spoke, clearly expressing his approval. When his dark-eyed gaze swung to Ella, his expression turned stony. He abruptly turned, drank from the spring, and then followed the warriors to the horses for closer inspection.

Ella rushed to the spring. She dropped to her sore knees at the edge of white rocks, cupped her hands, and brought water to her mouth. Most of it ran through her trembling fingers. She flopped down and lowered her head, her lips touching cool water. She drank in gulping swallows, choked and coughed, and drank again, at once sensing this moment would be etched in her mind forever. Without water she would soon die in this arid land, and the warriors had made certain their thirst came first.

A moccasined toe nudged her. She did not react, and was kicked for ignoring the probing foot. Ribs hurting, she winced but made no sound. She looked up. Her captor stood over her. He gestured impatiently to a waiting pony. Still she did not obey him.

The warrior reached down and

grabbed her forearm, yanking her to her feet. She lashed out with her free hand, trying to claw the eyes out of his painted face. He ducked away. Instead of anger, he showed a moment of triumph in his gleaming eyes, as though proud of possessing a spirited creature.

The warrior was quick and strong. He lifted her from the ground, thrust a hand between her thighs, and hefted her over the pony's back. He mounted a second horse. He gave Ella's pony a swat, and it trotted away to catch the others. Ella grabbed two handfuls of mane and held on.

She glanced back at her captor. He eyed her. She understood his silent message: To attempt escape or to fight him were pointless. If she tried, she would earn another beating for her trouble.

Ella drew a deep breath. She looked ahead. The water had refreshed her. Her head cleared. She was not without hope. Her father had survived the attack, and he would come for her. She knew that beyond all doubt. And she knew the trail left by a herd of horses on barren earth was impossible to conceal. Her father was probably tracking them at this moment, rushing to save her.

While she did not understand a word exchanged between the warriors, the tall one with a single feather in his hair was clearly a leader. When he lifted a hand in a silent signal, Ella's captor and two other men drove the stolen horses deeper into the barren sand hills. Her pony followed.

She looked back. Warriors led by the tall man turned away. Heading in a wide half-circle, those men and their mounts disappeared, concealed behind a hill overlooking the spring.

3

Four hours in the saddle under a blazing sun had taken a toll on Peter Howell. The plodding gait of the mule had chaffed his legs until every step of this critter brought pain. He wrapped the reins around the saddle horn and grasped it with both hands, pushing upward to take some weight off his sore buttocks.

He looked ahead. Now he lagged seventy-five yards behind the other riders. Half an hour ago he had only been fifty yards back. He saw sweat-soaked backs and salt-rimmed hats. The sun bore down on them, yet Earl Campbell seemed tireless. Howell figured the man would ride that mule into the ground before giving up, and then he would probably push ahead on foot, musket in hand, jaw set.

Howell understood. God willing, he would muster superhuman strength, too, if his Christina had been taken. He tried to ignore the pain and summon up new strength. He did not have to be a frontiersman to know that tracking the raiders was the easy part of the pursuit. The herd of stolen horses left a broad trail on dry land cut by gulches and shallow valleys. Howell watched the horizon ahead, as well as left and right, searching for sign — horse droppings on the ground, a sudden flight of birds, shadows at the crest of a hill, any movement in a bleak terrain to give away the enemy.

He saw nothing, yet, as Earl had commented during their last rest stop, they had reason to be encouraged. Herding horses was not easy work. While these mules were anything but swift of gait, their relentless stride set a pace the savages could not maintain.

Early in the chase Howell noticed the bachelors had held their guns at the ready. Their necks were craned for some glimpse of savages, but as time wore on, shoulders sagged and musket barrels dipped. Finally they shoved the heavy weapons into scabbards and devoted their energies to simply staying in the saddles. They dismounted only to water mules or study horse droppings. Under this sun, manure dried quickly, and the last pile they had examined had been damp.

Howell's mule lagged farther behind. Repeated kicks did no good. As much as he hated to do it, he knew what must be done. Before the rescuers rode out of earshot, Howell cupped his hands to his mouth and broke the silence.

'Earl!'

Campbell's head snapped around. Alarmed to see Howell so far behind, he turned his mount and rode back to him. The bachelors halted. They swung down and walked, stretching arms and backs while working kinks out of their legs.

'Don't know what can be wrong with the beast,' Howell said. 'I have shown him no mercy.'

Earl pointed to the right front leg. 'Lame. The critter's gone lame on you.'

Howell leaned forward and looked down. The leg was cocked at the knee.

'You ride on,' Howell said to his friend.

'I'll follow as best I can.'

Earl shook his head. 'Go back, Peter. You don't want to be caught out here alone.'

The two men stared at one another in silent disagreement. Howell made no argument, but he did not turn back, either.

'I reckon you know,' Earl said at last, 'that I can't order you to do anything you don't want to do. But you and I both know it makes good sense. Go back.' He added with a brief smile: 'Mister Buell Harris often said the savages out here fear firearms. We'll rout them with a volley or two from our muskets, and pick up Ella Mae.' With a nod to the injured mule, he went on: 'Likely we'll catch you and this slowpoke before you're in sight of the wagons.'

Peter Howell watched Earl turn his mount and rejoin the others. Pulling off his felt hat, he wiped sweat from his face while Earl took up the chase, with the three young men following close behind. Soon they were out of sight beyond a sandy rise.

Surrounded by silence broken only by the mule's pained breathing and the creak of saddle leather, Howell wrestled with his conscience. Truth be known, he had been bone-deep scared from the start. He had dreaded to think what would happen if the five of them overtook a war party outnumbering them by three to one. His decision to join the rescue party was solely a matter of duty to his friend. That, and sheer determination had brought him this far.

Now Howell looked around. Of course, Earl was right. This was wild, unmapped terrain, populated by savages. He should go back. It only made good sense.

Howell turned the mule. All he had to do now was backtrack. He would probably be in sight of the wagons by sundown or earlier. That certainty carried him along for a few paces. Then he yanked back on the reins. Muttering to himself, he called upon God in his heaven. He turned the mule to follow the four men, and kicked the critter, hard.

'Get moving! I beseech you! One jack-ass to another . . . get a move on!'

* * *

Through that long hot afternoon Ella clung to the pony's mane while her captor and two warriors herded horses. She recognized eight or ten Morgans owned by Levi Case. Others were saddle mounts belonging to various settler families.

The land flattened, stretching into a vast plain wrinkled by gulches. Grass grew out there, too, patches of green vegetation marking springs and bordering small, twisting creeks reflecting the blue sky. She heard an excited shout and saw a warrior point southward with his bow.

Ella shaded her face. The sight before her could not be real. The brown prairie seemed to shift and move, undulating like fabric on water. Squinting, she made out dark, horned heads and brown humped backs. The unbelievable sight was a herd of bison, hundreds of the great beasts moving shoulder to shoulder, nose to tail, as though bound together into a fluid, seamless mass. The warriors smiled at one another as they rode on, skirting the edge of the herd.

Through the day she often looked back, peering through a dust cloud churned by hoofs, a cloud she knew could be seen for miles. Yet the afternoon passed with no sign of rescuers. Tears sometimes ran from her eyes, but she wept in silence and kept her head up. Her captor ignored her.

Ella closed her eyes. She had always thought of herself as her father's girl, not for any lack of love for her mother, but it was her father who held her gaze, whom she had most wanted to please since early childhood. She had no doubt he would come for her. If not this hour, then the next. She longed for the moment of reunion, the moment she would run to him, the moment her ordeal ended.

Memories swept through her mind. The notion of leaving Baltimore for a gold strike on the frontier vaguely labeled

'Pike's Peak,' was one that had shocked her. At supper her father had read an article in the *Baltimore Sun*. The writer graphically described egg-sized nuggets in creek bottoms, free gold ready to be scooped up by the finder. Fortunes were being made almost daily in glacier-cold waters coursing through the cañons of the central Rocky Mountains. Such claims went unchallenged, readily swallowed by men suffering through a financial panic on the Eastern seaboard.

Earl Campbell's habit had been to read aloud from the newspaper, and, as Ella had grown older, they discussed subjects ranging from local politics to events in Europe. On that evening when she had idly listened to her father reading the account of riches in the gold fields of the American frontier, she saw him put down the paper. Her mother had watched in silence. Those signals had meant a momentous event was upon the Campbell family. Ella could never have guessed what it was, any more than she could have guessed how much the course of their lives would be altered from that moment on.

'That is where I will go,' Earl Campbell had announced, his index finger stabbing at the newspaper. 'The sooner I reach the gold fields, the better.'

Ella had stared. Her mother, eyes rapidly blinking, had lowered her head.

The Campbell family had suffered during the Panic of 1857, a period of financial strife Earl had labeled 'these damnable economic conditions.' The first blow had been the sudden closure of the bank in Washington where a month earlier Earl Campbell had been promoted to head teller. Unable to find another job, he had moved his family to Baltimore on the advice of his employer. The bank president's brother owned an international shipping firm, Cogsworth & Steele, and the company was in dire need of a trustworthy accountant.

The job that had sounded so promising, a dream come true after the nightmare of losing his head teller position, took Earl to a shack on the end of a pier in the harbor. He had supervised stevedores during the night and kept company books by the dim light of smoky oil lamps. Long hours of breathing that smoke and damp air had brought on a chest-wracking cough. Worse, the pay had been less than promised. On top of these personal troubles had come rumors of secession by Southern states. Through his misery, the promise of a fortune in gold had stirred him, no matter how vague or fanciful.

'You won't go alone,' Millicent had said, lifting her gaze.

Earl had started to argue, but had seen a set look in a sweet face, and had given it up.

Ella had left close friends behind in Washington, and had made none in Baltimore. For her, the decision to leave had come easily. Caught up in the excitement of their decision, she had echoed her mother's words. 'We'll all go, Father.'

That had been the easy part. Reality had hit hard. Money had to be saved, somehow. Earl barely earned enough to make ends meet. All purchases for the westward trek — food, clothing, boots, hand axe, a used Hawkin musket with powder horn and bullet mold — left not one cent for life's pleasures, no matter how small.

Worse, possessions had had to be sold at great loss — maple chairs, table, and dining set, glassware, settee, beds, dressers, household items — all of them modest but for the silver tea service and place settings. These were heirlooms. Millicent's parents had brought them from Ireland, along with a lace tablecloth and linen napkins with carved ivory napkin rings, minor treasures that had been in her family for more than a century.

At first Earl had refused to sell them. He well knew their sentimental value to Millicent, and had insisted he would find room in a wagon box for them. Instead, he would sell his gold pocket watch, a wedding gift from his bride. What good, he had asked with a laugh, is a timepiece on the timeless prairie?

Raised voices had sifted through the

paper-thin wall separating their bed-
rooms. Ella had overheard her parents.
They were not so much arguing as they
were discussing their differences with
great intensity. Millicent had argued
the wedding gift represented their life
together, their future, while the heirlooms represented the past. As a legacy,
those heirlooms could be sold and the
money used to buy a wagon and team in
St. Joseph, Missouri.

'Besides,' Millicent had added, 'how
else can we ever hope to afford to buy a
wagon and oxen?'

In the long silence that followed, Ella
had known her father had relented. He
would keep his timepiece. The silver and
lace would be sold.

Seven months later the Campbell
family had been camping on the bank
of the Mississippi River. Like thousands
of others from every state in the Union
and most countries of Europe, they had
journeyed to the edge of the frontier with
little more than bare necessities, determination, and hopes for a better life.

Quickly Earl had discovered prices of provisions to be exorbitant. He could hardly believe a used Conestoga wagon with a new canvas cover sold for $100. Two yokes and two chains cost him $18, a whip $1, and oxen were priced at $60 a head, no dickering.

Earl and Millicent Campbell had shaken their heads in dismay. Other prices had been inflated, too: flour at $3 a sack; bacon for $1 a pound; bushel of beans, $2; star candles, $4; eighty pounds of salt, $1.50, and ten gallons of vinegar, $3.

'A seller's market gone mad,' Earl had complained after spending more than double the amount he had budgeted for necessities on the trail ahead. Without enough money, what would they do when they reached the Denver camp? Earl did not know. All he could do was press on, and hope to have enough cash to survive while he hiked to the gold fields.

For months Ella had heard of St. Joe, this 'jumping off place,' as though a dark void lay beyond the river's western bank.

She sometimes dreamed of falling, tumbling through cold darkness until she awakened with a start, her hands grasping the quilt pieced together by her late grandmother.

A shaggy and profane frontiersman, Mr. Buell Harris had been hired as wagon master. He would lead the newly formed wagon train into the setting sun. With more swearing and spitting than necessary, he had claimed to have made the trek many times, that he knew the trail, that he could sniff the air and locate water holes with both eyes closed.

Peter Howell had gathered the settler families and bachelors in a circle of prayer. Seeking blessings and Godspeed, he declared them to be members of the 'Brethren Wagon Company.' He called upon every man, woman, and child to act in unity and, no matter what their individual beliefs, to live by the Golden Rule. With that, twenty-seven outfits with livestock had been ferried across the river — this passage one last exorbitant expense thrust upon them.

By that time Ella and Christina had become fast friends, and the Campbells and the Howells had formed their own partnership of share-and-share-alike. So began their journey into the great unknown.

* * *

A setting sun fired the western horizon when the raiders halted at a stone outcropping, the sole landmark for miles in any direction. Four to six feet in elevation, this rock formation rose up like the wall of a great fortress in ruin. Water gurgled through knee-high grass at the base of the outcropping. Tails switching, the horses drank and grazed without restraint, with no need for them to be physically confined here.

Ella swung a leg over the pony's back and slid to the ground. Knees weak, she staggered upstream from the horse herd. At the grassy bank of the creek she dropped to all fours and lowered her face into it, feeling a caress of the soft current while she drank.

She lifted her head to take a breath, and caught an unwanted glimpse of her face in the water's reflection. She saw a wild creature, a sun-burned, haggard girl with an empty gaze, auburn hair dark and matted to her head. Plunging her face into the cool water, she was briefly submerged, and came up blowing. As the water rippled, her image fragmented.

Sitting in high grass with her chin pressed to her knees, she stared at the horizon, eyes fixed on the back trail of the raiders. This stone landmark could not be missed, and, of course, the stolen horses had left a broad trail of churned earth and broken sage. Her father would bring a rescue party to this place, soon . . . .

Her head jerked around at a dry, buzzing sound. The sudden warning came from the rocks where the horses had wandered while they grazed. The buzz of a prairie rattler sent them rearing, hoofs kicking. Two warriors warily circled a coiled snake. Instead of stoning it as Ella had seen settler men dispatch the poisonous snakes, they lifted the six-foot, writhing creature up by two long sticks, and carried it far downstream where they tossed it into the grass. They returned to the camp and knelt with Ella's captor, resuming their low-voiced conversation.

The savages did not start a fire, perhaps out of caution. But Ella noticed they made no attempt to hide or post a sentry. She took heart from their carelessness. Every minute spent here brought her father closer. She watched them pass a buckskin pouch, each one pinching dried meat and berries between a forefinger and thumb, and eating it. Ella felt light-headed, suddenly famished herself.

She had not seen that pouch before. A growing uneasiness crept into her mind. Food had been concealed here. That meant this was a planned stopover on their escape route.

Ella stole glances at her captors. Savages had been portrayed to her as little more than dumb brutes. But now it was clear their attack had been carefully planned. She realized the three warriors were not careless. They exuded an air of confidence that was impressive.

The warriors ignored her as shadows stretched across the prairie, the air still and hot as an oven. Ella looked down at her nightdress. Torn and filthy, it reeked of soured sweat. She lay on her side and drew her knees up, eyes closing. Low voices from the men and the soothing sounds of gurgling water slowly faded.

Ella believed she would only rest, but when a toe nudged her sore ribs, she realized sleep had caught her. Eyes opening, she saw her captor standing over her. The man knelt, one hand sliding under her neck while the other thrust between her thighs. Lifted up, she thrashed and fought in silent desperation as he carried her away.

4

Sweating in the heat and squinting against the harsh brilliance of the setting sun, Peter Howell tugged at his low-crowned hat. The salt-crusted brim shaded his eyes, but still the glare forced his gaze downward. He was guided by the tracks left by Earl Campbell and the three young men as well as the horse herd driven by savages.

Howell had lost none of his resolve, but as the hours dragged toward nightfall, he knew reality must be faced. This mule was too slow. If he did not catch up with the rescuers by dark, what would he do? He knew Earl would not risk a fire, and he had little hope of locating a camp in darkness. Worse, he might blunder into an encampment of savages.

The mule limped through a shallow draw and over a low hill. The sun went down, offering immediate relief from the glare. The air was still furnace-hot, but, at least now, Howell could sit straight in the saddle and scan the terrain without blinding himself.

He stood in the stirrups, arching his sore back. He felt an overwhelming sense of discouragement — and a growing fear. His plan to follow Earl on a lame mule seemed more foolhardy than bold now. He looked around. After coming all this way, turning back would be a foolish act, too. No matter which way he went, darkness would catch him, a man alone on this endless plain.

In the bottom of a shallow draw the mule shied, long ears twitching as he tossed his head. With a snort, he planted his hoofs. Howell lashed him with the reins. The mule did not budge.

Howell looked around, his eyes searching for some sign of a predator. He saw nothing but shriveled cacti and scattered tufts of prairie grass. Even with repeated kicks, the mule refused to move forward. It backed away from a sand hill ahead.

Howell dismounted. He drew his revolver, the gun heavy and unfamiliar in his hand. He recalled advice to the settlers from Buell Harris. The wagon master had warned them to be watchful for savages in hiding. Those lords of the prairies, he claimed, possessed the ability to hide in plain sight. The statement brought skeptical laughter from the settlers who were skilled hunters. It was no tale, Buell Harris insisted, and described his experiences in the far land. An Indian could remain still for hours at a time, he said, lying behind a clump of sage or a boulder, and a careless man could easily walk past without seeing the warrior — until too late.

Now Howell examined the terrain, watchful for warriors hiding in plain sight. The land was barren. He saw nothing. No sounds reached his ears. He was alone here, alone with a big, stubborn, lame mule.

Howell saw tracks leading over the sand hill straight ahead. He drew a deep breath as he left the mule. Cocking the handgun, he climbed, stiff-legged and saddle sore. Still hearing no sounds, he felt increasingly confident savages were not in the area, certainly not on the other side of this sandy rise. The thieves could not possibly keep two dozen horses quiet.

His boots sank into the churned sand. This rise came up out of the prairie like an ocean swell stilled for all time. As a precaution, Howell dropped to his knees near the top. He pulled off his hat and crawled forward, pistol at the ready. A damp scent drifted into his nostrils — water. He almost shouted the word. In this dry land the scent of water was palpable. A spring in the next draw could have drawn a coyote or wolf, he figured, and the scent had spooked the mule.

Howell crawled to the crest. He lay down. Inching forward, he raised up on his elbows. The gleam of the evening sky was down there. He had been right. Sky-reflecting water pooled around white rocks in the bottom of the draw. His gaze moved to the left. He blinked. Four mules lay on blood-soaked ground down there, dead, still saddled, already bloating.

Howell moved forward. He felt sickened by the sight before him. Sprawled on the ground to the right of the rocks were the corpses of four men. Stripped naked, all of them were slashed and mutilated.

Peter Howell stared, his mind numbed by the carnage. He knew immediately what had happened here. Earl Campbell and the other three men had ridden into an ambush. Attackers had struck from the high ground, raining arrows down on the men as they drank. Then they had moved in and cut their victims, slashing each man from throat to testicles.

His grip loosening, the revolver fell from Howell's hand. The scene before him blurred. In tears, he bowed his head, not to pray, but to retch. Bile from his gut burned his throat, as though he had swallowed fire.

* * *

Ella was lowered into the grass near the brook. Her captor yanked her nightdress away. He thrust a knee between her thighs and moved on top of her as he pulled away his breechcloth.

She found strength to claw at him while twisting her hips, writhing under his weight. She heard him laugh, as though encouraged by her resistance. She spat in his face. He drew his arm back and cuffed her, hard. She tried to claw him again, but he batted her arms aside.

Her left hand, knocked to the ground, touched a cool, moving shape, a coiling creature that emitted a dry buzzing sound. In the next instant, she felt stinging pain in her forearm. She shrieked, and clutched her arm.

The warrior leaped away. He ran, stopped, and ran again, fleeing from this place.

By starlight Ella saw droplets of blood swell from twin punctures in her arm. She instinctively pressed her mouth to the wound, sucked, spat, and sucked again. She lay still, breathing hard.

Dizziness and strange sensations

swept through her. The gurgling brook sounded like ocean surf. She thought she saw men approach; they stared down at her until their painted faces receded from her view like ghosts. She heard her own voice calling out. Somehow she had separated from her body and become another person. She saw herself, a body lying in the grass under a darkening sky, and the sky was filled with the faces of strangers.

Fragments of the past came to her mind in vivid images. She remembered her mother's tears at the funeral of her grandmother . . . she remembered winning a spelling bee at her school in Washington . . . she remembered a mean boy throwing dog dung at her . . . and then she heard her own voice pleading for a grave marker so her father would be able to find her remains . . . .

Distant thunder was not thunder at all, but the rolling sounds of hoof beats hard on the earth, and suddenly riders burst out of the gathering darkness.

Father!

Horsemen swept in at a gallop, stirring dust. Ella saw spotted ponies. She coughed. Voices reached her, men speaking a language she did not understand. Tears came to her eyes. She lay back. Slipping into a troubled half-sleep, Ella dreamed of swimming underwater, escaping in a pond bordered by white rocks. At once she yearned for her family, for her friend, Christina, for all that was familiar to her.

At dawn Ella awakened with a raging thirst. Sounds of water gurgling over stones brought the bizarre dream back to her mind, watery images that slid away when she sat up. Her arm hurt, swollen where the snake had sunk fangs into her flesh. She crawled to the creek and drank until she could hold no more.

The warriors broke camp before sunup. At first light Ella saw the tall one leading the others as they rode out, driving horses before them. Her captor came to her with two spotted ponies. He lifted her onto the back of one and swung up on the other. Ella grasped the mane as they followed the war party away from the creek gurgling at the base of the stone formation.

★ ★ ★

The lone figure made a strange sight. A shout went up from the circled wagons after a child spotted a man leading a mule that limped. The man drew closer. Then a name passed from one cluster of settlers to another, reverberating through them like a soft echo: 'Peter Howell . . . Peter Howell . . . Peter Howell . . . .'

When Howell closed the distance, he dropped the reins. The settlers stared, silenced by the sight of a corpse draped over the saddle. Levi Case spoke first.

'Preacher Howell,' he said.

Jane and Christina Howell ran to the exhausted man and embraced him. Both women sobbed with relief to see him alive. After one full day and half of another without him, dark thoughts had filled their minds. Now, his head hanging, Howell's narrow shoulders shook with his own weeping.

'Preacher Howell,' Levi Case repeated. 'What happened out there?'

Case was flanked by Jared and Jason, both lean boys, Jared with a patchy beard and scabbed pimples. Other settler men gathered. All of them carried handguns or shoulder weapons, but none ventured outside the circle of wagons.

'Dead,' Howell answered hoarsely. 'All dead.'

The corpse was slung over the saddle on the limping mule, partially covered by a thick brown saddle blanket. Case moved to the animal's side and lifted the sweat-stained blanket. The mutilated corpse was barely recognizable. Case leaned closer, tilting his head as he studied the ashen face.

'Campbell,' he said. 'Earl Campbell.'

In the silence that followed, all of the settlers seemed to realize at once who was missing. They turned, looking across the way toward the Campbell wagon. Millicent stood by the tailgate, hands at her sides, alone in the world as she stared at them.

'She needs us,' Jane Howell whispered. 'Oh, my Lord, she needs us.'

Jane started toward her, but Millicent abruptly turned and climbed into the wagon box, pulling the cover down after her.

★ ★ ★

Food and rest had revived Peter Howell by sundown. He had told the settlers of his grisly discovery, weeping anew as he spared no details of the mutilations in the aftermath of a murderous attack. Howell had described moccasin tracks in the sand. The raiders must have launched their ambush from a hilltop overlooking the spring. No shots had been fired. Flint-tipped arrows must have whispered through the air, he said, and found their marks while the men knelt over pooling water to drink and fill their canteens. Dead in a matter of seconds, the mutilations had obviously taken longer. The brutality of it all shocked and angered the listeners. Only a beast could find satisfaction in cutting open a dead man. Savages.

Howell had dug into hot sand with his bare hands, burying three corpses as best he could. He had pulled four arrows out of Earl Campbell's body. Howell decided to recover his friend's remains for a proper burial in full view of grieving friends and family, a funeral service he would minister himself.

Seven graves were dug into the prairie near the rutted trail. The corpses were properly wrapped in bed sheets and lowered into final resting places — Earl Campbell, Buell Harris, Clara Osborne, Roger Hayes, Ludwig Gustafson, and two other settlers who had died of injuries. None of the raiders had been killed or even severely wounded.

At the funeral service, men and boys stood hatless, hands jammed into trouser pockets or arms folded across their chests, faces set in anger. Women and girls wore long black dresses, several donning dark veils unpacked from trunks. Clustered together, the settlers listened to Peter Howell as he read from the book of Psalms and spoke to his gathered brethren.

"Our loved ones soar beyond earthly pain to find eternal peace in the lap of God Almighty. Tears of sorrow cleanse our souls. Our loved ones . . . good and brave . . . respected by all who knew them . . . loved by those who knew them best."

Millicent Campbell refused to leave her wagon. She did not acknowledge whispered pleas from the Howells or anyone else. In the morning, sunlight spilled across the brown prairie, the heat of day curling blades of buffalo grass and dulling the sheen of sagebrush leaves on gnarled branches.

Hot weather seemed to ignite rage. Last night and this morning, Howell overheard settlers calling for revenge and rescue. Several bunched around Levi Case, venting their anger while devising a plan for action.

'Gentlemen, here is what we must do,' Case said.

Howell watched in silence. Levi Case spoke with authority. Men listened to him.

'We must form a militia when we reach the Denver camp. With force of arms, we shall track down the murdering savages, effect the rescue of Ella Mae Campbell, and leave the bodies of those butchers to rot in the sun!'

Howell stepped away as the settler men shouted their agreement. Having gained a healthy respect for the enemy and the terrain, Howell alone understood the risks of the chase. Tracking the raiders would be dangerous, perhaps impossible, by the time men, armed and stocked with provisions, rode to this spot from the Denver camp. Howell said nothing, but he believed bold talk of revenge was bravado, hollow posturing among men venting their anger.

The immediate task was to continue the journey to safety. Revenge would come later, if at all. These people, united now in a wagon train company, seemed to be of one mind, filled with high purpose. Howell kept his own counsel, but believed they would separate upon reaching their destination. They had traveled a long distance under life-threatening conditions, sustained by the belief that the sooner they made their fortunes on the frontier, the sooner they could return home.

Howell heard an anguished shout. He turned and saw Jacob Osborne approach Levi Case and the group of men standing before him. Walking in long strides, Osborne drew up, demanding to be heard.

'Them savages,' Osborne said, 'wasn't carrying guns, was they? Well, was they?' A big man, and now menacing, his reddened face shone with sweat. Settlers eyed him uneasily, none willing to cross him. 'I'm asking ever' one of you. Who killed my wife?'

'Now, Mister Osborne . . . ,' Levi Case began.

He broke in: 'Nobody's leaving this

camp till I get my answer. Who fired the bullet that killed her?'

Case stepped closer, his sons closing in on his left and right. He tried to calm him. The big man cursed, thrust his hands out, and shoved him away. Case staggered, but quickly caught his balance. Jared and Jason brought their muskets to bear on Osborne.

Howell stepped between them. 'Put the guns down.'

The Case brothers glowered at him, neither moving until their father repeated the command. Howell turned from them. He faced Osborne and reminded him the settler men had agreed to leave this camp first thing in the morning.

'Jake, we must roll out just as we would any other day,' Howell said. 'We're vulnerable to another attack if we tarry.'

Jaw clenched, Osborne said nothing.

'Preacher Howell's right,' Levi Case said. As though speaking for the world at large, he added: 'Mister Osborne, a thorough investigation into your accusation will be made once we reach the

Denver camp. I assure you on my honor as a gentleman . . . .'

'I won't take no mealy-mouthed talk off you!' Osborne exclaimed. 'Just tell me one thing . . . .'

'Calm down, man,' Case cut him off.

'Calm down, hell!' Osborne shouted. 'I want to know who killed my Clara!'

Howell moved in front of him as Levi Case pulled his sons away. They turned, heading for their wagons with the older boy, Jared, shouting a last taunt.

'There will be no more fighting,' Howell said, loud enough for all to hear. 'Not among ourselves.'

Red-faced, Osborne still did not back away.

'Jake,' Howell said, 'with you or without you, we're leaving this place. Give thought to your children. They need you now, and they will need you more when we arrive in the Denver camp.'

At last Osborne agreed to yoke his oxen. In a voice choked with emotion, he said again he would not rest until he knew who shot his wife. Howell did not voice an opinion about the identity of the man responsible for the errant bullet. He did not know. He had not fired his handgun in the mêlée. He knew that much.

Howell thought more about it as he readied his team and wagon with the help of Jane and Christina. With all of the wild shooting in the darkness before dawn of that terrible day, Osborne was probably right about the slaying of Clara Osborne. Howell doubted the killer's identity would ever be known. And he wondered what good could come of discovering who had fired the fatal ball.

* * *

Late in the afternoon Ella saw snow-crested peaks on the western horizon. Her gaze was captured by the sunlight glinting off white snowfields and glaciers at high elevations, a faraway place in sharp contrast to the gray-brown prairie that was oppressively hot, lifeless, and endless. Three days later she felt just the hint of cool air wafting out of distant cañons. Dust devils lifted skyward, propelled by mountain breezes swirling into hot air rising off the prairie. She knew now their destination lay somewhere in those far mountains.

Her crazed mind had cleared from the effects of rattlesnake venom. Insane dreams no longer rushed through her sleeping hours. She had not forgotten them. In vivid dream images, her arm had swelled like a log, her eyes shed tears of blood, her fingernails curled into black claws. When she gave birth to a wrinkled creature with fire-red eyes, she awakened in a hot sweat.

Ella had believed she would die, had even called for death's deliverance in the worst of her seizures. But she had survived. She regained strength, and discovered unexpected value in her shrill cries and bursts of mad laughter. The warriors drew away when she rolled her eyes and fell to her knees before them, tumbling over and thrashing about on the ground. Her captor stayed away.

Escape was never far from her thoughts. She considered fleeing, but sensed she would not get far. Evenings, the tall warrior brought pemmican for her, and set a gourd of water at her side. Whether she was afflicted by madness or not, he had clearly taken an interest in her. Warriors would recapture her if she attempted to escape. Worse, she figured something had happened to delay her father. Her plan now was to bide her time, to await the moment, and escape when the opportunity presented itself.

Herding stolen horses ahead of them, the raiding party moved over foothills and into a labyrinth of cañons. Far away, these mountains looked dark blue by day, purple by sunset. Now Ella saw green pines and blue spruces, the mighty trees stretching skyward.

Wild creeks crashed through cañons, the roar of pounding water resounding off granite walls. Great pine forests were broken by stands of white-barked aspen trees. In places, open meadows lush with tall grasses were decorated with gem-like wildflowers. On the mountainsides, outcroppings of granite bore mica, a silicate mineral reflecting sunlight like tiny shards of a broken mirror.

Ella washed in numbing cold water and drank from pools where trout darted away to hide in long shadows cast by trees. The larger trout were caught bare-handed by laughing warriors wading to their knees, men who now shared the catch with their captive while the tall warrior, unsmiling, watched in silence.

Herding horses in these mountain cañons was hard work. Stragglers were constantly pushed to keep up with the lead animals, while others tried to break from the herd. The days passed with the warriors' march slowed by runaway horses. Ella could not remember how many days had passed since leaving the prairie behind, but one sunny noontime she smelled wood smoke. Forest shadows came to life when buckskin-clad sentries appeared among the pine and spruce trees.

Startled, Ella saw the men raise their bows in silent greetings. Ahead, the dense forest opened into a grassy clearing on the bank of a blue lake. She saw cone-shaped lodges, sixty or seventy shelters made of stitched hides and supported by smooth poles gathered at the top. And she saw savages, dozens of them, young and old. Women and girls wore simple garb fashioned from tanned hides decorated with beads and feathers. With dogs barking and children shouting their greetings, the war party arrived home in triumph. Warriors herded horses toward the shore of the lake, slowly, for all to see.

Women and children came running to their husbands, fathers, and brothers. They shouted until they saw the strange one riding with the warriors. Halting, they stared in silence, at once curious and disgusted by her nudity and unkempt hair.

Ella tried to pull her nightdress together. Much torn, the fabric was filthy. Under the gazes of savages, young and old, she was suddenly self-conscious. No understanding of their language was needed to know she was not welcome here.

5

Like a blanket of iron, tragedy weighed heavily. On the last leg of their journey, a collective fatigue settled over the men and women of the Brethren Wagon Company. Ten grueling weeks on the trail and one dawn of horror had left them in a state of emotional exhaustion. The settlers trudged to their destination, resembling a rag-tag army in a forced march.

Finally there came a last day, an end. The company that had formed on the eastern bank of the Mississippi River at St. Joe disbanded quietly on the western bank of the South Platte River. With no formal ceremony on the outskirts of the Denver camp, men shook hands and women embraced, many weeping as they whispered their goodbyes.

A few agreed to stay together for mutual protection in the gold diggings of mountain gulches. Others planned to combine their labors on plots of land, the sites of new farms to be plowed from raw prairie. As Peter Howell had privately predicted, no words of rescue and revenge were uttered here, no braggadocio, and even the name of Ella Mae Campbell went unmentioned as the settlers quietly parted.

The Denver camp was a ramshackle collection of open campsites, shabby tents fashioned from wagon covers, and squat log cabins scattered along the river. Slow-moving and shallow, the muddied waters of the South Platte were said to be too dirty to drink and too thin to plow. In the camp, livestock — cattle, goats, sheep — ran loose by day and were penned at night with chickens, ducks, and pigs. Muddy pigsties stunk of manure and urine.

The landscape was littered with the débris of abandoned campsites from last season — rusted barrel hoops and broken staves, cracked axles and ruined wheels, and charred logs where miners had wintered. Most had fled the cold winds. For those who stayed and toughed it out, the hot days of mid-summer buzzed with flies and the air reeked of human and animal waste.

Saloons, gambling parlors, and dance halls had been constructed of fresh-cut pine. Boards came from a new sawmill by the river, but in their rush to start businesses to 'mine the miners,' the lumber had been used before it cured. Under a hot sun, knots popped out of boards that bowed and warped, lending a tumble-down appearance to new structures.

Bachelors lost money in the gaming establishments, drank themselves into stupors in beer halls, and engaged in fistfights with strangers over disputes forgotten by sunup. Half sick and completely hung over, they headed for the storied gold fields early in the morning, gripped by a fever of greed. Eager to scoop up fortunes in gold nuggets, their plan was to move fast to the diggings, then they would return home, wealthy, long before the first snowfall.

Howell had not known what to expect here. He found the Denver camp to be wild and chaotic, and could hardly blame his friends for swiftly departing this vision of hell. Outlaw bands — most were failed gold seekers — moved between the Denver camp and gulches in the foothills like pirates roaming through port cities. Howell had seen these armed men on horseback observe arriving wagon trains with the flat stares of predators. Shootings and stabbings were common occurrences — one murder every night, folks said — and newcomers were routinely robbed by toughs who hid in thick brush near the river by day, slipping out at night brandishing guns.

No one called this lawless place a town. It was a camp, a stop-off for emigrants on their way to somewhere else. Gunfire and a foul stench only hurried them along. A few members of the Brethren Wagon Company stayed with Peter Howell in the Denver camp, fifteen men, women, and children bunched for common protection. The widower, Jake Osborne, and two widows, Millicent Campbell and Greta Gustafson, were among them.

Bernard Cleeve had managed to bring his wagons in with borrowed oxen. His three wagonloads of goods were snapped up by local merchants, and now he carried the proceeds in a money belt under his shirt. He had purchased four mules, and bellowed mightily at the price, at once knowing he had to pay the going rate, just as shopkeepers had been forced to pay his inflated prices. Armed with a holstered pistol, Cleeve camped near the Howell and Campbell wagons while waiting for a train of freighters to form up for the long trek back across the Great Plains to St. Joe. With a little luck, he could make a second crossing before the snow flew.

Jacob Osborne's wagon was close by, too. He was a man who had lost direction in life. Broken by grief, he had taken to muttering, and it was not unusual for folks to see him wandering by the river, talking to himself in a quiet, mumbling rage. Christina and her mother tended the Osborne children. They ranged in age from seven to fourteen, three girls and two boys. Greta Gustafson, who spoke no English, had joined them with four young children of her own. The widow had not shed tears, but as a stranger in a strange land she was timid. Afraid to leave the wagons, she held her children close day and night, like a hen protecting chicks.

Through it all, Levi Case had made no secret of his ambitions. With his sons on newly purchased saddle mounts, he roamed the prairie within a day's ride of Denver, at last finding graze on rolling hills and water in cat-tail-choked lowlands. He was eager to draw boundaries and register his LC brand.

The Case Ranch, Levi had declared, would one day be known throughout the nation and Europe for its purebred horses. The theft by savages was a setback, to be sure, but more Morgan horses were *en route*. Ranch hands were coming, too.

Case was charged with a larger purpose in life, for he meant to pioneer a renowned ranch just as his grandfather had founded the Case Plantation in Virginia a century ago. Horses were his passion. He would breed cattle, but only to sell beef locally as a means to finance his great ranch of the West.

Howell heard the man speak eloquently of his dream for prosperity in a new land. The ranch was more than a place for his sons and grandsons to live and prosper, Case declared, but a legacy for them to build on and pass to their own progeny.

Mail was turtle-slow, but in time Case learned his letters had been received in Virginia. He confirmed tradesmen and drovers were on the way with more loaded wagons. With pine trees felled, bucked, and hauled from mountain forests, Levi Case would build his ranch house and barns, and tame a wild land.

Some people wondered if Millicent Campbell had lost the power of speech. She worked in silence alongside Jane and Christina at their daily tasks of meal preparation and cleaning chores, just as she had labored side by side with them at campsites on the trail. But now, eyes downcast, Millicent rarely spoke and never smiled. Jane had to cajole her to eat as one would encourage a child. Millie had lost so much weight that she became bird-like with clothes hanging from her gaunt body. Christina expressed her fear the woman would die from lack of nourishment.

The thought had crossed Peter Howell's mind, too. He tried to talk to her, to carry on a conversation, with no success. He should not have been surprised. After the funeral on the trail, he had failed to persuade Millie to leave the camp marked by seven crosses fashioned from barrel staves.

'I must stay with my husband,' she had whispered to him at the time. 'I must stay until my Ella Mae returns. You go ahead, all of you. I shall be all right.'

Howell had called for volunteers. Settler men had roped the Campbell oxen, backed them to the wagon tongue, and yoked them. One of the bachelors had wielded a whip. He had popped it, and walked beside the team as the Campbell wagon rolled into line with Millicent inside, canvas wagon cover drawn shut, her sobbing cries almost drowned out by the sounds of wagons under way.

Now Howell realized that leaving her husband's grave marked the day Millicent Campbell had stopped talking. She sometimes spoke a word or two to Jane and Christina, nodded in response to queries, but rarely communicated with anyone else.

On foot, Peter Howell walked half a mile and mounted a rise beside the river. Overlooking the Denver camp from this bluff, he meditated for a time. Then he watched comings and goings. Not only had he never seen a place like this, he had never even read an accurate description of it. Smoke clouded the air over the campsites, and the ever-present stench of waste and garbage filled his nostrils. His mission, his reason for traveling to this hellish camp, was to minister to men and women far from home who hungered for spiritual nourishment. In time he hoped to found a church, believing that was what God had called him to do.

While Howell had not known exactly what to expect on the frontier, he had firmly believed he was prepared for adversity. Now on this grassy rise he stood before his maker, a humbled man. The truth loomed large and fearsome. He had not been prepared, not for the fatigue, not for the stress and endless exertion of the westward trek, and certainly not for the violent loss of life he had witnessed on the trail. Now in this camp, as folks casually stated, one man was murdered every day.

Howell returned to his wagon, knowing he must relate a matter of great importance to his wife and daughter. He had sought guidance in solitary prayer, and found it. He had not yet found the right moment to give it voice. At nightfall he gazed at his loved ones across a campfire. Leaping flames showed their tattered clothes and worn shoes. Fatigue lined their hollow-cheeked faces, particularly Jane's. The rigors of the trek had exacted a toll on her, deepening lines in her face.

Regret swept over Howell. From the start he had wanted to make this trek alone, offering to send for them after his church was established. They would not hear of it. Touched by their loyalty, he had consented. But if he had it do over, he would not have allowed them to leave a comfortable and safe home in Delaware to venture into the great desert.

Only fools mistook regret for thought. Howell knew that, and pushed heartache away. Gazing at his wife and daughter, he still did not know how to tell them. The only certainty in his mind was that no matter how much he prayed silently and beseeched aloud on that hilltop, the answer was always the same: Ella Mae Campbell had to be found. She had to be freed from the savages.

★ ★ ★

The fire in the center of the teepee was tended by the ugliest creature ever born. Ella watched the bent old woman, thick-bodied and foul-smelling with greasy hair hanging past her shoulders. Bare-footed, the crone wore a shapeless garment of animal hides. Her bronzed face was prune-wrinkled, eyes dark as coal, nose broad and flat, and one yellowed tooth was visible in a mouth, hanging open.

Completely naked now, Ella was not bound, but clearly she was confined here. Twice she had moved toward the flap, and both times the crone whirled to face her, moving with surprising speed and grace as she raised a switch in an unmistakable threat. For the first time in a long while, Ella had to smile, if only briefly. For she had little doubt she could overpower this old woman. At once she knew a fight would accomplish nothing. Without clothing or shoes, where could she go?

Late into the night Ella heard the steady *thump-thump, thump-thump* of drums, a hypnotic beat accompanied by chants and ceremonial cries of deep-voiced warriors. Thoughts of escape crowded into her mind again. She feared they would kill her in some savage display of human sacrifice, but as hours passed no one came for her. When the crone draped a buffalo robe around her, Ella stretched out, asleep the moment her eyes closed.

In the morning the old woman brought water in clay pots, and, after hand signals failed to communicate her message, she stepped close and vigorously washed Ella from head to toe and every private place in between. Ella was surprised by her strength. Maybe she would not be so easily overpowered, after all. Later the crone brought a beaded buckskin dress and flung it at her.

Ella put it on, glad to be clothed again, and she was surprised by the buttery softness of the leather. It felt good next to her skin. She watched the old woman's gnarled hands as she made a pungent stew of root vegetables and chunks of dark meat. The woman demonstrated eating stew with a horn spoon, her movements exaggerated, as she clearly believed Ella was not capable of understanding how such an instrument should be used. After the meal she brushed Ella's hair with a comb fashioned from the tail of a porcupine.

Ella was allowed to leave the teepee only to relieve herself. Even then she was tied to the crone like a leashed dog. Outside, the two of them were followed by curious children to a stand of waist-high willows near the forest. Ella tried to guard her privacy, but was watched by silent onlookers while answering nature's call.

The days passed bright and sunny as Ella observed blue skies through the smoke hole of the teepee. She could not see what was happening outdoors, but from the sounds out there she was aware of a camp pulsing with activity. It started early each morning when fires were stoked and children led ponies to graze near the lake. As the sun came up, hungry babies cried, children shouted, and dogs yapped and growled in play.

Ella heard the voices of men in their comings and goings, sometimes laughing, often speaking in earnest outside the teepee. A lull came at midday. Later, with the last light of day, families gathered, ate, and talked before retiring to their lodges. Ella listened to voices fading into nighttime silence, feeling a great, peaceful quietude broken only by the hoots of an owl or the calls of coyotes.

At first Ella felt compelled to count the days, to keep some sort of record of time's passage during her captivity. She often thought of her father. Sometimes she believed he would come for her. Other times she feared something had happened to him, that he would never come for her. Marks scratched into dirt to count the days only deepened her despair. She rubbed them out with the heel of a bare foot, preferring to let one sunny day flow into the next.

At noon the flap was thrust open, admitting a scrawny old man with thin, white hair. Almost nude, his dark body was smeared with ashes. He carried a rattle made from a turtle shell, and at his gaunt waist hung the furry tail of a squirrel and a leather pouch.

Ella drew back, her eyes fixed on this bony old man. He sang in a low voice while shaking the rattle in a deliberate beat. Low and slow, he circled her while reaching into the pouch to draw out ashes by the handful. Still chanting, he sprinkled the sooty ashes on the ground around her. Then, as quickly as he had come into the teepee, he backed to the flap, and ducked out.

Ella saw the crone staring after him, clearly in awe of his powers. Outside the village was quiet even in midday. Ella closed her eyes. A shiver coursed through her.

* * *

The saloon was windowless, nameless, and nondescript, a low, flat-roofed dead-fall built of peeled cottonwood logs and chinked with mud from the river. Peter Howell found the place near a bend in the South Platte, having been directed here by Jake Osborne. The watering hole was a 'nest of Rebs,' by Osborne's description.

Now Howell paused in the open doorway. His eyes slowly adjusted to dim light cast by oil lamps with soot-stained chimneys. Dark and cool inside, the saloon reeked of stale beer, spat chaw, and soured sweat. Howell saw a dozen or fifteen men standing at a plank bar along one wall. In the rear, beer barrels were stacked two high.

'Preacher Howell.'

Howell half turned. He heard the familiar voice, smooth as molasses, but could not yet see the man. He peered through shadows clouded with pipe and cigar smoke, and ventured inside two more paces. In the gloom back there, two men sat at a gaming table where they kept company with a long-necked amber bottle flanked by two shot glasses. Howell approached them, remembering something about Levi Case.

Before embarking on the trail from St. Joe, the men of the Brethren Wagon Company had voted to leave all spirits behind, unanimously agreeing liquor brought nothing but trouble. They faced enough adversity on the trail ahead without adding the devil's brew to the list. All agreed, to a man, except Levi Case. He had argued against this decision, and lost. At the time Howell had suspected the man gave up too easily, that he kept a supply of whisky or rum in his wagon for he had smelled it on the man's breath a number of times. Without real proof, though, Howell had said nothing. Besides, if Case kept his liquor to himself, what could be gained by searching three freight wagons at gunpoint? Howell figured that action would have been required to subdue the man and his two sons, and he had no stomach for it.

'Preacher Howell,' Levi Case repeated now. 'Pull up a chair.'

Howell moved closer, seeing the second man more clearly. He was a clean-shaven gent with fine features, a thin mustache, and trimmed sideburns. A meerschaum pipe was clenched in his teeth.

'This is Mister Aaron Cahill,' Case said by way of introduction, 'the proprietor.'

'Pleased to make your acquaintance, Mister Cahill,' Howell said, and gripped a fine-boned hand in a handshake. While he pulled out a chair and sat at the table, Case informed the saloon man how they had come to know one another. When he finished, he turned to Howell.

'Have a drink for what ails you.'

'What ails me will not be cured by whisky,' Howell said.

Case studied him. 'If I am any judge of character, and I fancy that I am, you are here to settle unfinished business.'

Howell met his gaze.

'And I suppose,' Case went on, 'that business concerns the rescue of Miss Ella Mae Campbell.'

Howell nodded. 'I need some men. Armed men with strong mounts.'

'Of course,' Case said. A knowing look crossed his face, as though he had expected this conversation and had rehearsed his part. 'Lord knows I dearly wish we could return the Campbell girl to her mother's embrace. I wish I could recover my Morgan studs and mares, too. But as you know all too well, the desert is vast and uncharted, known to savages just as the ocean is known to sharks . . . .'

In no mood for a speech, Howell broke in: 'Mister Case, I intend to bring her out.'

Levi Case paused. 'Preacher Howell, assuming you are able to get up a militia, how will you find the girl?'

'I'll begin where she was last seen,' he replied. 'The trail left by the horse herd will not be difficult to follow in dry terrain.'

'Sir, with all due respect,' Case said, 'what is your military experience?' When no answer came, he went on: 'You are doomed to fail. To my way of thinking, more loss of life is a price too high to pay.'

'I am surprised to hear you speak this way,' Howell said, 'after giving your word as a gentleman to lead the effort in raising a militia to rescue the girl . . . .'

Case lifted a hand. 'Sir, you challenge my honor in a public place. In my grandfather's day we would have been obligated to settle this with pistols, with Mister Cahill as my second. However, this is the frontier where men are plain spoken. With that in mind, here is your answer: Within hours of our arrival in this god-forsaken camp, the men of the Brethren Wagon Company departed like shadows in the night. You know that as well as I do. Isn't that true, sir?'

Howell eyed him. He did not say so, but he suspected Levi Case had never planned to raise a militia at all, that the man had made an empty promise simply as a convenient means to an end — reaching the Denver camp as soon as possible, where he would enact his plans for building a ranch under the LC brand.

'As a man obedient to God,' Howell

said, 'I must try.' He turned to the saloon man. 'Mister Cahill, I am here to ask you to pass the word to men of good character. I seek mounted men who will ride with me for the purpose of rescuing Miss Campbell from the band of savages who took her.' He added: 'I can offer no earthly reward.'

Cahill took the pipe from his mouth and replied in a soft drawl: 'Preacher, word of the attack and that poor girl's capture spread through this camp hours after your arrival. Fact is,' he added with a glance at Case, 'that's how I learned this fellow Virginian was in your wagon company.' He thrust the pipe back into his mouth and talked around it. 'I've heard talk. Men hereabouts declare it to be a fruitless search, and a deadly one as Mister Case says.' He drew on the pipe and blew out a cloud of smoke. 'For what it's worth, preacher, I shall pass along your request to men of my acquaintance . . . no riff-raff. Perhaps some will prove me wrong and ride with you, after all.'

Howell returned to his wagon, now filled with doubts as his nostrils filled with stench. He knew what he must do, even if he had to do it alone.

Did God send me to this place to die? A flock of chickens dodged his boots with panicked squawks and a great flapping of clipped wings. Ahead, he saw his wife and daughter, waiting for him by the wagon.

6

'Yer driving a hard bargain, ye stinkin' chief. Damned if ye ain't.'

Ella came awake with a start. Had she heard that growling voice outside the teepee, or dreamed it? Then she heard it again.

'I thought we was friends, ye stinkin' bastard.'

'Help!' Ella shouted hoarsely. Her voice was weak from disuse. She had hardly spoken since the day of her capture, and for a moment she forgot how to form words. She raised up and drew a deep breath.

'Help me! Help me!'

The crone scurried to her side, grabbed her, and tried to cover her mouth. Ella bit her. The old woman pulled away, looking at the palm of her hand in alarm.

'Ye got a white girl in there, chief? Do ye?'

Ella moved to the teepee flap and

threw it open. Before she could lunge through it, she was grabbed from behind by gnarled, claw-like hands. The weight of the old woman pulled her down, and they both fell to the robes covering the ground inside the teepee.

'Help me!' Ella shouted again. She rolled away from the old woman and scrambled to her feet. She screamed again.

'What kinda wildcat ye got in there, chief?'

Light streamed through the triangular opening when a shaggy, hatless man leaned in. He pushed tangled hair away from his face, and swore in amazement.

For a long moment Ella merely stared. She could not find her voice. Then the man ducked down and came in. He straightened up, hands on his hips. He was followed by several warriors, her captor among them.

'Who are ye?'

Ella winced against his foul body odor. He was short, thick-bodied like a bull, his bovine face square and pocked. She gasped, trying to fill her lungs and speak at once.

'My name . . . my name is Ella . . . Ella Mae Campbell. I was taken by savages . . . from our wagon train. Wagon master is Mister Buell Harris . . . attacked . . . on our way to the Denver camp . . . attacked . . . .'

The shaggy man swore again. 'I git your meanin', girlie. Ye was stoled, warn't ye?'

She nodded, glancing past him to see her captor's dark stare.

'Yeah, I git your meanin',' he repeated. He squinted and lowered his voice as though that was a cunning way to conceal his message from the silent onlookers. 'Maybe I can help ye, girlie, but I gotta go slow and easy. Plumb slow and easy. These bastards, they could slit my throat in a flash iffen they so took a notion.'

Ella eyed him. The man wore dark blue wool trousers and a dirty, patched shirt of red flannel with bone buttons. A large revolver was holstered to the right side of a cartridge belt with an antler-handled knife sheathed on the left.

'Who . . . who are you?' she asked.

'Name's Zebulon,' he replied. 'Zebulon Becker. I trade with these here stinkin' savages . . . skinnin' knives, hatchets, glass beads and such fer tanned hides.' He gestured with a wave of his hand. 'This here mountain lake, it's their summer ground. Right now they's happy and peaceable, in a tradin' frame of mind, ye might say.'

Zebulon Becker threw a false smile over his shoulder, and lowered his voice again as he leaned close to her. 'But these here savages, they can turn war-like in the blink of a damned eye. That's what I'm a-telling you, girlie. They'll turn on me if I make a move to haul ye outta here.'

Ella whispered: 'Please help me.'

'Dead, I won't do ye no good,' he said.

'Perhaps . . . perhaps you can trade . . . .' Her voice faltered. 'Trade something for me.'

'Such as what?' he asked. He studied

her. 'I'm pondering. Your pa . . . would he be a man of some means, as folks say?'

She met his gaze. She sensed that if she seized on the obvious lie, the man would not believe her. She shook her head slowly, thinking of another lie.

'My father works for Cogsworth and Steele, the international shipping firm. He has come out West to establish the company in the Denver camp.'

Becker let out a harsh laugh. 'A trader, huh? Jest like me!'

My father is nothing like you, she thought. Aloud, she explained: 'My family is not wealthy, Mister Becker, but Father will show his gratitude if you escort me to the Denver camp. I am certain of that.'

'Gratitude, huh?' he said. He paused. 'I like the sound of that. Maybe somewheres in the neighborhood of . . . uh, maybe somewheres in the neighborhood of five hunnert dollars, gold.'

'If that is the proper amount,' Ella said, 'I will tell him five hundred is our agreement.'

Becker nodded slowly. 'Might cost

more, girlie.'

'I understand,' she said, trying to hold her voice steady. 'My father will reward you handsomely, I know that much.'

'Handsomely,' he repeated. 'Now, there's a fancy word. Ain't that a fancy one?'

'Can you help me, Mister Becker?'

He rubbed his bearded jaw. 'I'll see about that. I'll see about that.'

Ella looked past the trader when a shadow darkened the light streaming in through the open flap. She saw a young man duck in. He stood and edged past the warriors. In profile his features resembled the tribesmen — high, pointed cheek bones and thin lips. But his black hair was cropped short, and he wore a buttoned cotton shirt, wool trousers, and boots, the garb of a white man. She heard him converse with the warriors in a low voice, and saw Becker turn to face him.

'What're these stinkin' bastards telling you, 'breed?' Becker asked.

The young man turned and faced

them now. Ella stared. She saw one eye socket closed in a youthful face, the skin sewn together like pieced fabric. Fine scars creased that side of his jaw. His one-eyed gaze swung past her. He answered in perfect English.

'They say you're a savage, Zeb, not to be trusted.'

Becker laughed without humor. 'Someday I'm a-gonna bury my knife in ye, 'breed. Bury it to the damned hilt.'

'These warriors are wondering about you,' he said.

Becker's false smile faded. 'Wondering what?'

'What kind of scheme you're cooking up with the white woman,' he replied.

'Tell 'em to go to hell, ever' damned one.'

'Indian people don't believe in hell.'

'Then you go to hell, 'breed,' he said, 'and report back to the heathens.'

The one-eyed young man ignored him. He turned to Ella. 'The elders call you Woman Spirit of the Snake. They say a powerful spirit lives in your body.' He asked: 'You were bitten by a rattlesnake?'

Ella nodded, still shocked by his appearance and his command of English. 'Who . . . who are you?'

'White people call me Seth Carter,' he replied. 'A long time ago, a long way from here, I was taken in by a family named Carter.'

'These here savages,' Becker said with another hollow laugh, 'call him One-Eyed Skunk.' Laughing again, he reached out to cup Ella's breast in his hand.

'Leave her be, Zeb,' Seth said. 'Leave her be before Many Bears gets the notion you want her.'

'Hell, I don't want her,' Becker said, withdrawing his hand. 'You tell 'em that, 'breed.'

Seth turned away. He spoke to Many Bears, the stocky warrior with a web of lines on his face and white paint under his eyes. Then Seth moved past the warriors. He bent down, swiftly ducking out of the teepee.

'Damned 'breed,' Becker muttered.

'Who is he?' Ella asked.

105

'You don't want nothing to do with him.'

'Why not?'

'Because he's a god-damned 'breed.'

'But what is he doing here? Where did he come from?'

'Hell, I dunno. He was born to some squaw and a half-breed trapper, both dyin' from smallpox when he was a kid.' Becker drew a ragged breath. 'The 'breed, he claims he got schoolin' back in the States, somewhere or other, until he run off. He never took to the white man's ways. Indian ways, neither. He roams these here mountains like a lone wolf. Now and then he swaps pelts to me fer goods.' Eyes narrowing, he added: 'Mark my words, girlie. Don't trust a 'breed.'

But Becker must have taken Seth's word, Ella thought, for the trader turned and left the teepee. Warriors filed out after him. Many Bears was the last to leave.

Ella brought her hands to her face. She fought tears. That last remark from

Zebulon Becker rang true. She could trust no one.

★ ★ ★

Sunday dawned hot, and the clear blue sky over the prairie promised more of the same. The Howells prepared for services on the bluff overlooking the South Platte and the Denver camp. Yesterday, Peter had made the rounds of saloons and gambling halls, enduring catcalls while inviting all within earshot to attend Sunday morning worship services.

Donning his broad-brimmed, low-crowned black hat now, Howell stood in bright sunlight, a black-covered Bible pressed to his chest. His wife and daughter wore black dresses with black lace trim and pearl buttons, polished black shoes, and simple hats, black, too.

Howell had carried his well-traveled trunk up the slope. On level ground he opened it, pulling out a brass cross with a weighted base, a stack of hymnals, and a hand bell. He closed the trunk and placed the cross on the lid. Jane stacked hymnals on either side of it. Christina stepped aside, bell clutched in her hand. At a nod from her father, she lifted the bell and rang it vigorously. Then they waited, three figures clad in black as they stood behind a cross gleaming in sunshine on the hilltop.

This tableau was observed from a distance by a lone figure in a tattered brown dress and cracked shoes, the footgear unlaced and unpolished. Millicent Campbell sat on a folded quilt in the shade cast by her wagon, the same quilt her mother had sewn for a baby named Ella Mae. Today, Millicent had refused the Howells' invitation to attend worship services.

In the next half hour Peter Howell greeted single men and families who trudged up the slope to stand before the cross. Most accepted a hymnal from Christina. A few brought Bibles. Among the gathered faithful were the widow Gustafson and her children, Jacob Osborne with his children, and the merchant, Bernard Cleeve.

In his sermon, Howell addressed the twin evils of temptation and greed, identifying them as sins that took the form of gambling and drinking in the Denver camp. He read scripture from the first book of Peter, explaining with a smile that the words did not come from Peter Howell, but from God himself, the deity speaking through the disciple who once had betrayed Jesus. "Blessed is the man that endureth temptation. For when he is tried, he shall receive the crown of life." If Peter found redemption in the eyes of God, Howell informed his congregation, then so can sinners of today.

'With purity of heart, my brethren,' he concluded in a booming voice, 'ask God for forgiveness! Ask, and you shall reap rewards beyond all riches!' He added in a low voice — 'For eternity.' — and bowed his head.

Jane and Christina led the singing. Howell's standard joke was that he lived up to the promise of his surname, a musical gift limited to a howl. His singing voice was useful for hammering the fear of God into the skull of any man stubborn enough to believe he could withstand it. By contrast, he announced, the duets of his wife and daughter were angelic, music of the spheres in this barren desert so far from home and hearth.

After the service Howell shook hands with each man in attendance, and described the abduction of Ella Mae Campbell by savages. Husbands and bachelors alike listened in quiet sympathy, but none volunteered to aid in the girl's rescue.

'Preacher, I've quit my drinking.'

Howell turned to find Jake Osborne standing close behind him. The big man had waited to speak privately.

'From this day forward,' Howell said, 'your mind and body will be free from the bondage of demon liquor.'

'I aim to brace for winter,' Osborne went on. 'Next season I'll take my children back home. I've got family in northern Indiana, and I figure the children belong with relatives.' He added: 'They still dream of their ma dying . . . reckon I do, too.'

Howell watched his florid face, realizing the man was, in his own way, building to a point.

'Since we landed in this foul camp,' Osborne continued, 'I've heard talk in saloons. Ever' man has heard the tale of Ella Mae Campbell, the killin' of her pa by savages, and so on. Ever' man says we could ride for months without tracking down the raiders who took Ella Mae. And if we did stumble onto their camp, why, we'd die a long and horrible death for our trouble.' He paused. 'That's what men are saying.'

Now Howell understood, or thought he did. 'Jake, I appreciate your counsel. But God has spoken to me. I simply cannot rest until I have expended every effort to bring her out.'

'That's what I figured,' Osborne said. Again he paused. 'I aim to ride with you.'

Caught by surprise, Howell was speechless for a long moment. 'Jake,' he said at last, 'your children need you . . . now more than ever.'

'No more than your wife and daughter need you, preacher,' the big man said.

'Jake . . . .'

'Now, preacher, no amount of jawing will change my thinking,' Osborne said. 'You're not the only man on the face of this old earth to hear the word of God.' With a cock-eyed grin, Jacob Osborne strode away with his children lining out behind him like goslings.

Howell turned and saw Jane. She averted her gaze. He knew immediately she had overheard the exchange, and it had pained her. She had always supported him, even when it meant leaving friends and worldly comforts behind to travel into the far reaches of the frontier. In seventeen years of marriage she had suffered with him and had triumphed with him, from his first church to his last. And she had neither fussed nor held him back that awful dawn when he had ridden with Earl Campbell and the rescue party.

But this was different. Her delicate

chin quivering, Jane could not hold her tears. 'Peter, you advised Mister Osborne to think of his family. Will you? Will you think of me? Christina? Your mission here?'

'Daddy,' Christina whispered as she came into her father's arms. 'Daddy.'

★ ★ ★

In the evening Seth returned, entering the teepee in the company of Many Bears and the tall warrior. The warrior's name, Seth told her, was Eagle Feather. After them, four elders of the tribe entered — 'old man chiefs,' according to Seth. They sat around the fire in the middle of the teepee. A long-stemmed pipe was fired and passed among them.

'They asked me to translate,' Seth said, sitting behind her. He told her to face the circle and keep her head down, eyes averted. 'They want you to know the right ceremonies have been performed. Don't stare at them. If you do, they will think you are hostile.'

'Seth,' she whispered, 'I must get out of here . . . .'

'Don't fight them,' Seth said. 'I'll try to help you later. For now, go along.'

'But . . . .'

He lifted a hand for emphasis, his expression stern. Ella remembered Becker's fear of these savages, and complied. She gazed at the flames in the fire ring. At last one elder spoke, then another.

From Seth, she learned they called themselves the People of the Blue Lake. Most were Cheyennes, but Arapahoes lived with them. The tribe's warriors were known as Bow Strings. The old medicine man had sprinkled ashes in the teepee and voiced a chant to purify her. Now that she was cleansed, Many Bears was prepared to trade her to Eagle Feather.

Ella remembered Eagle Feather had brought water and pemmican to her while on the trail. Many Bears had shown fear of her after she was bitten by the snake, but Eagle Feather did not appear wary of her insane screechings. Now, in

114

exchange for seven horses, Seth told her, she would become the property of Eagle Feather.

Ella forced herself to exhibit no signs of resistance. She did not stare at any of these men. She bowed her head, trying to fill her mind with memories of family and home as a way to control her emotions. Trance-like, she sat perfectly still with her eyes closed. When she finally opened them, the men were gone as though she had sent them away by force of will. Seth was gone, too.

She was not alone. The crone sat on the far side of the teepee, watching. She grimaced in arthritic pain as she got to her feet. She came to Ella, hesitated, and then rested a gnarled hand on her shoulder.

Thoughts of escape had filled Ella's mind since the moment of her abduction from the wagon train. Her hopes had briefly soared when she first heard the trader's curses, and then again she felt a wave of excitement when Seth said he would try to help her. But as days passed with no sign of him, the inevitable conclusion came to mind, the same conclusion she had reached when she sensed something must have happened to her father that had prevented a rescue attempt.

Fear came first. She was alone, fearful. But she steeled herself, her determination strengthened by a growing certainty that she could rely on no one, that she would have to help herself. She knew what she must do. And she knew, if she waited until Eagle Feather came for her, escape from this encampment might be impossible.

As she thought about her daily routine, she knew her best opportunity came when she was taken out to the willows by the crone every evening. At first they had been followed, watched by curious onlookers, particularly children. But the novelty had worn off. Not even young children gave them a second look now. And even though she was tethered to the crone by a length of woven rawhide, the knot was carelessly tied.

Ella ate heartily, slipping pieces of jerked venison under her dress when the crone turned her back. At dusk, the old woman took her outside. The western sky over high mountain peaks glowed with the last light of day when they walked into the stand of willows outside the camp.

Ella glanced back. The People of the Blue Lake had gathered before retiring to their lodges. Men, women, and children left behind their endless chores — scraping stretched hides before tanning; catching, gutting, and hanging native trout in willow racks to dry; carving fresh meat from an elk carcass; gathering wood for morning fires.

Ella saw this in a glance over her shoulder. She took a deep breath as she reached the willows. The tether drew tight. She made a pretense of wending her way deeper into the thick growth of willows, as though seeking privacy.

Ella looked back. The old woman cast an annoyed look at her, but followed in shuffling steps. Ahead, level ground dropped off to a slope of loose shale. Ella had glimpsed this terrain before — a steep slope of broken rocks where nothing grew. As she approached it now, the crone grunted and firmly drew back on the tether. Her meaning was clear: go no farther. We must return to camp before dark.

Ella disobeyed. She yanked on the tether. When the old woman pulled back, Ella rushed her. Caught by surprise, the crone staggered backwards, waving flabby arms to regain her balance. She was not agile, and Ella quickly loosened the tether while moving behind her. Planting her hands in the middle of the crone's humped back, she shoved.

The old woman stumbled and completely lost her balance. She fell over the side, landing flat on her stomach with a pained groan. She half rolled and skidded down the steep slope of loose shale. Ella saw fear and amazement in her upturned face, a frightened old woman sliding down to the bottom with her gnarled hands bleeding from attempts to grasp shards of rock.

A wave of regret washed through Ella as she realized what she had done. The crone could have shrieked and cried out for help. But except for groans, she remained silent, grimacing through her pain. With a last look into the dark eyes in the wrinkled face down below, Ella turned and ran.

7

That evening, by firelight, Peter Howell moved close to Millicent Campbell. He spoke to her in a low voice while her gaze remained fixed on the flames. She seemed to shiver, as though cold on a warm evening, and pulled a quilt around her shoulders.

Howell had no way of knowing how she would react to his plan for rescuing Ella Mae, and had postponed this moment as long as possible. He had convinced Jane and Christina that God had called him, or, at least, had convinced them his mind could not be changed. Now he watched Millicent's face as he spoke to her, the doughy, wrinkled skin cast in fire-borne shadows. This woman was fragile physically and emotionally. Now she was silent, unmoving.

Howell had been prepared for an outburst from her, for soul-wrenching sobs, for gratitude, or even a demand to accompany him. He had not expected this. Millicent simply looked into the fire, empty-eyed and still as stone, with no outward reaction to his words.

In the darkness before dawn, though, when he was ready to depart, he found her waiting by his borrowed mare. She hugged him. With her arms tightly wrapped around him, she pressed her face to his chest. She neither cried nor uttered a sound. She broke away and scurried back to her wagon.

After a last embrace and hushed good byes to his wife and daughter, Howell swung up into the saddle and eased out of camp. He had told his family an early start would save him from some of the heat on the prairie, but in truth he meant to avoid another encounter with Jake Osborne. The man was mad to think he should leave his children for this trek, yet Howell knew he could not talk him out of it. Better to leave quietly before the camp stirred.

He followed the rutted trail by star-light. Nearly every possession he carried was borrowed, from the mare and saddle and bridle to a canvas sack filled with donated food, four canteens of water, and a brass telescope loaned by Bernard Cleeve. He carried his Bible in a rucksack tied behind the saddle. That belonged to him. So did the octagonal-barreled Remington revolver holstered on his cartridge belt, a gift from a church member back home. The weapon had not been fired since he had squeezed off practice rounds on the bank of the Mississippi at the St. Joe crossing. It had kicked like a Missouri mule and belched out a great plume of powder smoke. Howell flinched every time he had fired it, and did not know if he could hit any target, much less kill man or beast with it.

His failure to raise an armed militia to rescue Ella Mae had troubled him deeply. He had prayed over it, asking God for direction, and at last knew he must ride alone. It was the only real choice left to him, and he took that as a sign from above. Most of the men he had spoken to had declined outright to take part in a rescue mission. Some had scraped a boot toe in the dirt while studying the ground, allowing they might make the ride if others joined in. There was safety in numbers. But in the end only three men promised unconditionally to ride with him, and two of them reeked of alcohol. One did not own a firearm.

By his reckoning, Howell figured he had a better chance of avoiding discovery by savages if he traveled alone. Two or three men would be of little help, sober or not. Certainly he did not need Osborne.

In those hours Howell's thoughts evolved into a plan. First, he would locate the camp of the raiding party. Then, with Ella Mae's whereabouts known, he would return here. In his best ministerial bellowing, he would cajole and berate able-bodied men of the Denver camp, shaming each one into joining him in a forceful and violent rout of the savages.

Riding due east now, Howell squinted against the rising sun. Heat quickly intensified like a stoked stove. By mid-morning he had emptied two canteens to slake his own thirst and to water the mare from his hat. At noon he refilled the canteens with murky water at a crossing. He ate, rested, and rode on. The rhythmic *clip-clop* of hoofs, the squeak of saddle leather, and occasional ringing of a bridle chain were the only sounds in this still prairie — until the vast silence was broken by a shout.

As though startled out of a nap, Howell stiffened. He turned in the saddle. He saw a figure in the distance. Remembering the telescope, he yanked the instrument from a saddlebag and pulled it open. He raised the eyepiece to his eye and leveled the lenses. The rider back there was a large-framed man on a small, brown horse, a man alone who waved a felt hat over his head.

Howell lowered the telescope. It was Jake Osborne.

★　★　★

Heart pounding, Ella felt unfamiliar braids bounce against her shoulders, hair that had been greased and braided by the crone. Tears sprang to her eyes as she thought of the old woman sliding down that rough slope, her gnarled hands raw, her ancient face showing fear and amazement — and betrayal.

Bent low now, Ella caught her breath. At a lope she followed the growth of willows on the crest of the rocky slope. The forest ahead yawned like a ragged, dark shadow. She hoped it would swallow her.

The thin light of evening gave her some cover. Sooner or later an alarm would be sounded in the encampment. By then she hoped to be half a mile away, perhaps more, and moving fast.

Run by night, hide by day. That was her plan, a plan made in haste and desperation. At some point, she would follow a creek downslope. Water would sustain her, and lead her toward the wagon road, and from there to the Denver camp.

She had not considered encountering a sentry, and nearly panicked when she glimpsed a lone warrior kneeling at the edge of the pine and spruce forest. She halted and dropped to her hands and knees, breathing hard, choking back sobs. Dressed in buckskin with a trade blanket draped over his shoulders, the sentry knelt fifty or sixty yards away, his back to her. He was armed with a bow and quiver of feathered arrows.

Ella raised up slowly, just far enough to see his profile. He was motionless. He had not seen her. But if she moved closer to the trees, he would either spot her or hear her. In the next moment a shrill whistle brought him to his feet. He drew an arrow from his quiver, looking left and right. Ella forced herself to be still as his gaze swept past her. A second night call reached him. He turned and sprinted toward the encampment.

Ella stood. She ran into the trees, knowing her absence had been discovered, the alarm sounded.

Like an enormous beast, this forest seemed to breathe cool air, exhaling damp and wild odors. Her first instinct was to run as fast as her feet could carry her, but, after tripping on a downed branch, she realized the darkness that offered protection also represented danger. If she injured herself, her escape would be slowed, perhaps doomed when pursuers came for her.

Even so, fear drove her. She fought her instincts to flee headlong. By force of will, she moved deliberately, feeling her way like a blind woman through this dark forest while shouts came from the encampment.

In those first minutes of freedom she tried to move in a consistent direction, a straight line, even though she was uncertain if that direction was east or west, north or south. For now she did not care. Somewhere she had read that, when lost, a person can panic and hike in a widening circle without knowing it. A circle would take her back to the tee-pees by the lake.

She reached a break in the forest. Hesitating, she eased into a starlit clearing. Lush with knee-high grass, this meadow was surrounded by pines. She started to cross it, halting when her moccasined foot sank into cold water. A brook flowed through tall grasses.

She dropped to all fours and drank thirstily, like an animal. She had not realized how thirsty she was until that moment. Standing, she heard water sloshing in her stomach as she jogged across the meadow to the cover of trees on the other side, the night air cooling her sweating body. In the black forest again, she held her hands straight out, walking slowly while warding off needled boughs.

For a time desperation and fear overcame her fatigue. She was determined to keep moving, to rest later, but found herself stumbling. Her knees buckled. She tried to press on, but could not. When she reached another small clearing, she halted, and sat down. Eyes closing, she lay on her side on dried pine needles. Even though this bed was prickly, she fell asleep.

Startled, she opened her eyes. She

looked up through towering treetops to a sunny blue sky overheard. The hour was long past dawn, perhaps well into mid-morning. Suddenly aware of movement to her left, she nearly shrieked until she saw the antlers of a bull moose. The big animal stepped into the clearing and sauntered along the treeline, unaware of her.

Ella saw a pool in the meadow. An oval of water mirrored the morning sky. She moved to the muddy bank, sending the moose trotting away, and drank until she could hold no more. She recalled the spring surrounded by white rocks in the prairie far from here. At night her dreams took her back to that place where water pooled in a dry land.

She bit off a piece of stringy jerky she had brought from the lodge. She chewed, eyes closed. A soft sound reached her. Too late, she realized it was the sigh of an animal. She turned to see a horse, a black and white pony on the edge of the forest, the rider's dark eyes fixed on her.

★ ★ ★

'I wanted to see her grave one more time, Preacher.'

Peter Howell heard sorrow in the voice of Jake Osborne when he spoke those words. Riding side by side, they were silent until the big man said he had considered recovering Clara's remains for burial 'back home.' He mulled that over, at last admitting such a plan was not workable.

'I just hate leaving her out here, that's all,' he said. 'I know she's gone ... I know she's in heaven and all ....'

'Clara will live in your heart,' Howell said, 'and in the hearts of your children. For all eternity.'

Osborne idly nodded, but made no other reply. Howell eyed him. More than a grieving widower, the man was troubled. No longer a morose drinking man wandering through the Denver camp, he was sober now, sober and clear-headed. Howell wondered why his brow was furrowed.

Howell was relieved when Osborne did not insist on riding with him to track the raiding party. He had no right to tell him that he could not do as he wished. But he was adamant about the two of them pursuing savages. The notion was dangerous, one that could get both of them killed.

The two men rode on, alone on the wagon trail that had led countless gold seekers and settlers to the frontier. Not a straight line, the trail was serpentine as it led from one water hole to the next. On horseback they took short cuts and covered ground in three days that had taken the ox-drawn wagons ten or twelve.

They reached the prairie campsite neither of them would ever forget. It was a bare patch of prairie marked by blackened fire rings, broken wagon wheel spokes, and all of the usual débris of a heavily used campsite. This site was also marked by crosses fashioned from barrel staves.

Osborne wept the moment he saw the graves, his mighty shoulders quaking.

He rode slowly into the camp, drew rein, and dismounted. Hat off and head bowed, he dropped to his knees at his wife's final resting place. His hands covered his bearded face, and he cried in deep, gasping sobs.

Howell stood by quietly. This place brought a surge of memories back to him, as well — death, fear, sorrow, rage. He also recalled the good humor among settlers in the days prior to the attack. With assurances from Buell Harris their destination was drawing near, they had peered at the horizon ahead in search of the first view of the Rocky Mountains. The memorable day came when Cleeve had passed his telescope around. That dark line on the far horizon, he had said, was a range of mountains, the storied Pike's Peak country, even though in truth the mountain bearing that name was far to the south.

From that day on, the sun had seemed not quite as hot, the wagons had rolled without a breakdown, and the sore hoofs of oxen had not slowed their progress. All had been well until the darkness before dawn of that unforgettable day.

Now Jake Osborne built a campfire. Howell fried thick slabs of bacon and heaped molasses-soaked brown beans into the hot pan. Osborne boiled water and made coffee. After eating, he got up. Tin cup of coffee in hand, he walked in a widening circle around the campsite. His gaze was downcast as he studied the ground. Howell asked what he was doing.

'I'm trying to recollect where our wagons was circled that night,' Osborne said. He pointed to the ground. 'Mine was about here. Wasn't it?'

Howell nodded. 'I suppose so.'

'Campbell and Gustafson wagons was over yonder,' he went on. 'And Cleeve's freight outfits was over there, side by side, next to the three wagons of Levi Case.' He turned to him. 'Right so far, Preacher?'

Howell replied with another nod.

Osborne pressed him: 'See what I'm driving at?'

'Can't say I do, Jake.'

'It's plain as day.'

'What is?'

Osborne cocked his arm in sudden fury and threw the cup at an imaginary target, coffee sloshing out before the cup hit the ground. Bouncing, it rolled across packed earth with a clatter and stopped where he had pointed.

'The musket ball that killed my Clara! It came from over there . . . right there! That spot where Levi Case and his sons was bedded down!'

Howell stood and approached the big man.

'Preacher,' Osborne went on angrily, 'I took to drink to stop the ghosts from preying on my mind. Now I don't drink spirits no more, and I'm still thinking about the killing, thinking about it plenty. I even dream about it. I know it's true.'

'What is?'

'Them Case boys was shootin' all over the place,' Osborne said. 'I asked Bernie Cleeve and other folks. Ever'body agrees on that. Most of the shootin' came from there. My wagon was in the line of fire. Look for yourself. Plain as day, Preacher.'

'Jake . . . .'

'My Clara,' Osborne replied with tears welling in his eyes. 'My Clara, she was killed by Levi Case . . . him or one of his sons.'

★ ★ ★

Ella feared more for her life now than at any time since the first moments of her abduction. Alone in the teepee with her wrists and ankles lashed together, she awaited a beating — or worse.

The warrior named Eagle Feather had caught up with her in that sun-washed meadow. He slid off his pony's back. After a brief chase on foot, he caught her and brought her back to the encampment by the blue lake.

The villagers had turned out, silent and watchful. Ella was reminded of a funeral procession she had once seen. Onlookers had stared in silence at a black hearse with windows covered by black curtains. Now a line of savages stared at her as though seeing a doomed woman.

But she was neither beaten nor starved. Thrust into the teepee by the warrior, she was left there, alone and bound. Food and water were brought to her in the evening by Eagle Feather. While he untied her wrists, she watched his angular face and dark eyes, trying to divine his thoughts. He left, closing the flap behind him.

After he was gone, Ella wondered what had happened to the crone, if she had been punished for having allowed her to escape. She wished she could ask someone — yet at once she had no desire to find out what had happened to the old woman. Anger pushed away her compassion. She was still determined to escape. Running away from these savages filled her mind even as she fell asleep.

In the morning the crone came for her. Ella sat up. Looking at the thick-bodied woman, she saw no obvious injuries from a beating. The dirty, claw-like hands were still bloodied, and loose folds of flesh under her chin were scraped raw — injuries sustained from Ella's shove that had sent her sliding down the rocky slope.

Gazing at the old face now, Ella felt a measure of sympathy for her. She wished she could somehow communicate her feelings, woman to woman. But no signal was possible. The crone averted her eyes. Loosening the strap that bound Ella's ankles, she took it off and led her out of the lodge to the willows.

Ella walked gingerly. She was barefooted, probably to discourage her from fleeing, and this time they were watched by women and children. When the crone escorted her back to the encampment, they passed by the teepee where she had been confined. Surprised and filled with suspicion, Ella drew up, or tried to. The crone pulled her along.

Ella was again aware that she was the object of curiosity in the tribe. Old men and women stared. Women scowled. One spat. Children kicked dirt at her. Ella was taken to another lodge, this one near the center of the village. She saw a red sun painted over the entry flap. The crone signaled her to bend down, and shoved her inside.

Ella staggered into the teepee. Catching her balance, she straightened up. The crone stayed outside, and closed the flap. Eagle Feather reclined on buffalo robes by a small fire in the center of the teepee.

Ella saw him regarding her. He motioned to a robe at his side. She considered defying him, but recalled Zebulon Beck's fear of these savages. She also remembered Seth's whispered advice when he had cautioned her against putting up a fight.

Now she met the warrior's gaze. She forced herself to sit on a soft buffalo robe next to him. For the first time she noted his skin was smooth, in this light the color of damp earth.

Eagle Feather lifted a small parfleche. He paused, his eyes on her. Then he thrust the hard-sided pouch at her. Ella lowered her eyes. There was no mistaking his intent. She looked into the flames,

138

and made no move to accept the gift.

Eagle Feather made a sound. Still, she did not move or look at him. After a long moment, he opened the pouch, clearly expecting her to pay attention. Ella watched him now. He took out beads of blue, red, and green glass, a necklace of elk teeth, an awl, flint blade, and a gold pocket watch.

A shiver coursed through her body as she stared at the round timepiece. She reached out suddenly and snatched it from him. Turning it over, she pressed the stem. The cover flipped open, revealing a clock face with Roman numerals. On the inside of the cover she saw the familiar inscription:

Earl
Beloved Husband
August 22, 1843
Millicent
Devoted Wife

★ ★ ★

At dawn they shook hands in parting. Jake Osborne had agreed to return to the Denver camp. He understood Howell's strategy. A lone rider had a better chance of tracking the savages without being observed than two men on horseback. Osborne also agreed that his children needed him. The two men promised to meet in the Denver camp upon Howell's return. Until then, Osborne offered to look out for Jane and Christina.

Howell paused before he turned to his mare. 'No man escapes justice in the hereafter, Jake. Remember that.'

Osborne eyed him. 'Is that your way of saying I got no business going after Levi Case?'

'It is my way of saying,' Howell replied, 'that no man should nurture revenge. Vengeance belongs to the Lord.'

Osborne offered no other comment. He bid Howell good bye, swung up into the saddle, and rode away.

Leaving the campsite, Howell rode past upended shards of sandstone to the dry ravine that had concealed the war party. He looked back. He saw Jacob Osborne following the wagon trail toward the Denver camp, a big man on a small horse.

Howell crossed the dry ravine. He rode under a hot sun, hour after long hour, to the spring surrounded by white rocks — the site of the massacre. A putrid stench filled the hot air.

To his horror, Howell saw that animals had chewed on the corpses, dragging them from the sandy graves. He saw ashen flesh gnawed to snow-white bones. Birds pecked at carrion. The sight and smell of this hellish place made him retch and weep at once.

He sought comfort in his belief the men were beyond agony, that they had found peace in heaven. Even so, Howell wished he could re-bury the bodies. Any civilized man would show such respect for the dead. But without tools, digging deep graves was impossible. Covering the remains with handfuls of dry sand achieved nothing. He whispered a prayer, filled his canteens, and rode away.

Howell crossed endless swells of the sand hills, the hot sun pounding him into drowsiness. Tracks left by the herd of stolen horses were clear. As he rode, he tried to fathom savages who murdered innocent men — and then slashed them with such ferocity.

Were the savages no better than wolves? Nothing in his background or religious education had prepared him for the sight of mutilated victims. The brutality of it was more than he could understand, just as stealing a young woman from her family was beyond his ken. Were they human at all?

Howell pondered this question while the borrowed horse plodded across a barren prairie. Perhaps the savages were dark angels performing the work of Satan on earth. If so, he thought, they must be sent back, every red devil dispatched to the fires of hell. For eternity.

8

All this time Ella was sustained by a belief that her father, even though somehow prevented from rescuing her, was alive. One day he would find her — or she would escape from her captors and find him. Dreams of a reunion were shattered when she stared at the gold timepiece in her hand.

She lashed out at Eagle Feather, trying to scratch his eyes. He was caught by surprise. Her fingernails raked his face. He grabbed her. Pinning her arms at her sides, he twisted her upper body until she fell back with him on top of her.

Sobbing, she was powerless to escape his weight and the pungent odor of his body. For a long time he held her in a hard embrace. She remembered her pretense of madness on the trail, and suddenly laughed through her tears. She laughed and cried hysterically, knowing her voice carried beyond the teepee.

Eagle Feather let her go. He rose up to his knees. He eyed her warily, clearly baffled and at once angered. She suspected he knew this bizarre behavior was an act, but he did not know how to stop the shrill cries.

He observed her for a time. When she quieted and rolled her eyes, shivering, he grasped her wrist. He stood and yanked her to her feet. Shoving her outside, he took her back to the empty lodge on the far edge of the encampment. The crone waited there, her eyes downcast in his presence.

The warrior pulled his prize into the teepee, shoved her down, and spoke harshly to the old woman. She obeyed, quickly binding Ella's wrists and ankles. Eagle Feather tested the knots. Finding them to his satisfaction, he left.

Ella lay on her side, eyes closed, exhausted. In her mind she still saw the gold watch. She could hardly bear to think of it. She knew her father had not lost it. Eagle Feather had not traded for it. The timepiece in the savage's parfleche could mean only one thing — her father was dead.

Ella was as certain of that as she could be without actually having seen his body, and the awful certainty bore down on her. She felt it like a great, suffocating force, a weight pressing the last breath from her chest like the warrior lying on top of her. She believed that he had meant to subdue her, nothing more. He could have killed her. She knew that. She also knew she would not have resisted, for she did not want to go on. She did not want to draw another breath. She wanted this ordeal to end, and now wished for her last and final escape.

She lay still, emulating death to bring its final peace closer to her heart. She did not weep. Her tears were gone, as though they had flowed from a vessel long since dry. Thoughts of her mother drifted into her mind. Where was she at this moment? Did she know her husband was dead? Did she believe her daughter was gone forever? Would she stay on the frontier, or would she return home without learning Ella's fate? Or did Millicent Campbell have any choice in the matter?

Ella did not know the answers. All she knew for certain was that she would never eat again or drink again. No one could force her. She would grow weak, shrivel, and die. Victory would be hers. Eyes closing, she prepared herself for endless sleep.

The campfire in the teepee flickered and died out. Familiar sounds of village life in the evening reached her, voices fading as families went into their lodges. Darkness fell. The air chilled. For Ella, the night was long, silent, and lonely. Was death like this? Instead of slipping into the dark and unending silence that she craved, her eyes opened. She heard a sound. A scraping noise came from behind her.

Ella did not turn toward the sound. She did not even move when sinew popped like violin strings. The scent of evening air came to her, air that smelled of the lake. She heard a rustle behind her.

A moment later one warm hand closed over her mouth. She tried to squirm away.

'It's me. Seth.'

Ella lay still. His hand released her. She was aware of a night shadow at her side — and the glint of a knife blade. Then she felt the touch of Seth's hand again. His fingers slid over her buttocks, moving down her leg to her ankle.

He leaned over her. In a sawing motion, he cut the bonds. Then he freed her wrists.

Ella sat up. She turned to face this shadow in near darkness. 'What . . . what are you doing . . . ?'

'Shhhh,' he whispered, sheathing the knife. 'Come with me.'

'But . . .'

Off to her left, another shadow stirred in the teepee. She made out the thick form of the crone moving toward her. The old woman brought heavy moccasins and leggings. She put them on Ella and backed away, a rounded form fading into darkness.

'She wants to help you,' Seth whispered.

Ella felt a pang of guilt. 'Why?'

'In her youth,' Seth replied, 'she was taken from the Utes, stolen from her family. Come on.'

Ella got to her feet — or tried to. Her thigh muscles were sore and tight from running through the forest. She staggered, bumping into Seth. He steadied her. For a moment she clung to him, feeling his warm body against her.

'Stay close,' he whispered. 'Camp dogs know my scent. Yours, too. They won't bark much.'

Remembering her escape attempt, she whispered: 'Sentries.'

'The lake is unguarded,' Seth replied. 'Bow Strings believe their enemies, the Utes, will come through the trees.'

He moved away. He pulled the hides apart where he had cut the stitching. Ella bent down, feeling the ache in her legs again. She went through the aperture.

Outside, she straightened up and looked around. Lodges were bathed in dim starlight. This one was set aside, the closest to the shore of the lake. Seth whispered to the crone before he came out, alone. He moved past Ella. She followed him until halted by a growling dog. She stood still. Another dog approached, both crouched as they stalked her.

Seth came back. Closing the distance, he gave each dog a kick and sent them skulking away. He grasped Ella's hand.

They moved past a cluster of ponies to the shore. Soft mud turned to water, or it seemed to as Ella walked toward the undulating starshine on the surface of the lake. A vast gleam of water stretched out before her, the mud flat reeking of its wet odors.

Seth halted and whispered: 'Take off your dress.'

She stood still, not answering.

'Wet buckskin is like cold iron,' he said. 'Take off that dress and carry it.'

She did not move.

'The water's ice cold,' he whispered, 'but this is the only way we can go without getting caught.'

'I . . . I can't swim.'

'We'll stay in the shallow part of the lake,' he whispered, 'and make our way to that rock over there.'

She looked where he pointed, but saw only a dark shape on the distant shore.

'Move slow. Don't splash.' He undressed and held his boots and trousers out of the water.

Ella paused, afraid, knowing her only alternative was to go back. She pulled off her dress, and draped it over her shoulders. Naked in the night, she followed Seth.

Her feet went numb. As they waded into deeper water, a chill shot through her body like cold lightning. She thought she could not bear it, but knew she had to. She remembered her wish to die. Hours earlier it had been a desire keenly felt, yet quickly abandoned when hope had come to her. Freed, she was eager to find her mother.

Seth pulled her into waist-high water. Stepping gingerly on rounded rocks, they made their way around the perimeter of the lake away from the encampment. Ella lost all sensations in her lower body. One ponderous step at a time, she thrust a numbed leg forward, then the other, walking with no more feeling in either extremity than in a pair of stumps. Her exposed chest was covered with goose-bumps. Worse, the cold seemed to crawl deeper into her body, as though freezing her from within.

With water up to his elbows, Seth slowly angled toward the dark outcropping. Ella followed, gasping now. She feared she would go under. She might have, too, but she saw Seth reach a stone formation on the edge of the lake. He climbed out, his wet legs gleaming in starlight. Turning, he reached down and gave her his hand.

Ella grasped it and was pulled out of the water. In the dim light she saw him smile, and suddenly felt self-conscious. He turned away while he pulled on his trousers and shirt.

She put on the buckskin dress, and followed him across the flat top of the stone outcropping. Open ground lay ahead. Seth moved as swiftly as a deer, sprinting through the meadow toward a stand of pines fifty yards away.

Ella could not keep up with him. He disappeared in the trees. She halted. Treetops stretched up to stars shining in a black sky. For a moment she wondered if he had planned to leave her behind all along, that she would fend for herself from here on. She had no way to survive, no tools, no food, no landmarks to help her find her way.

Alone for those moments, an odd sensation swept over her. It was not fear. She had lived with fear since that dark morning of her capture by Many Bears. This sensation was a feeling of calm detachment, as though embracing the reality of her own death had freed her from the tyranny of fear. She no longer wished for death's release. Now she was eager to live, eager to find her mother.

Movement caught her eye. In the next moment a lean shadow came to her.

Seth reached out and grasped her

hand. He turned and led her into the forest, this time moving at a slower pace.

★ ★ ★

Next to an attack by savages, Peter Howell believed the vast, dry prairie represented the greatest threat to his safety. A man alone in a barren land was dependent on his mount and a full measure of luck in finding the next water hole. Howell had a trail to follow, and that fact saved him. He was no frontiersman, but had only to follow the dim imprints of hoofs, a wide trail leading from one source of water to the next.

From that spring pooling amid white rocks, Howell followed the tracks of the stolen horses through the course of the day. The trail led him out of desolate sand hills across a plain. In the evening he spotted a fringe of tall grass ahead. Drawing closer, he saw a natural wall of gray granite. He heard the brook before he saw it. So did the mare. Ears perked, she broke into a trot. Water gurgled over stones. Now he saw a brook winding through grass growing along the base of that granite formation.

He dismounted and pulled off the horse's bridle. Man and beast drank thirstily. Howell submerged his face into the cool water and came up blowing. He rubbed his beard-stubbled jaw vigorously. Then he drank again, gulping until he could hold no more.

Howell got to his feet. He was weary, yet exhilarated. He looked around. Then he walked through grass littered with horse droppings and the leavings of other animals. He jumped, startled by sudden movement underfoot. A diamondback rattlesnake slithered away, the six-footer avoiding the boots of an intruder.

Clearly the raiding party had camped here. Tracks showed they had moved on, bearing west, straight toward the mountains. Howell hobbled the horse, and bedded down in high grass, asleep instantly. At dawn he drank again, ate, and rode out.

Over the next three days the trail led

him over low foothills marked by tufts of sun-browned grasses and clumps of pear cacti, a trail easily followed until he entered the maze of mountain cañons.

Fire and ice, water and wind — ancient forces of nature had carved stone and uplifted landforms, leaving great rifts in rugged terrain. Some cañons were deep and dry; others bore rushing waters that crashed against boulders in a constant roar. Some were beautifully forested; others were cut from igneous rock with sheer cliffs on either side.

The trail disappeared. Howell wandered, believing he would cut the tracks of horses sooner or later. But he did not. Desperation drove him. Where could the savages have gone? The steep-sided cañons he explored narrowed into deadends, sending him back the way he had come, back to scale another mountain, to enter another cañon. The deepest one claimed his horse.

Howell had led the mare along a narrowing ledge high above the cañon bottom. He meant to come out on a rise he had seen in the distance, and from there resume his search for tracks. He took out the brass telescope and glassed the area, hoping to see horses, a wisp of smoke, or any other sign of the savages. He did not.

Too late, he noticed the ledge narrowed. He halted. He tried to back the mare. Shying, her shod hoofs slipped and then scraped frantically against stone. In an eye-blink she was gone. Howell watched helplessly as the mare slid over the side, tumbling into a free fall to her death, three hundred feet below.

Howell stared at the churning water down below. He stood in shocked silence while the current pushed the dead horse downstream. Caught in swift water, the panniers spilled out their contents, quickly washed away. In an instant Howell was left with the clothes he wore, the telescope, his holstered revolver, and nothing more — no rain slicker, no canteens, no food, no spare ammunition. In despair, he turned and walked back the way he had come.

In the following days hunger twisted his thoughts and filled his mind with false images. Sometimes he believed he was searching for the wagon train. Other delusions brought his wife and daughter before him, vivid images of Jane and Christina smiling, gesturing for him to join them . . . .

After a great deal of wandering and backtracking, he followed a game trail into a meadow. He surprised a small herd of elk. Drawing his revolver, he fired off six rounds at the retreating animals, each bullet missing the target. Plumes of gunsmoke thinned and drifted skyward as the bulls tipped their heads back and trotted into the dense forest. They were followed in orderly fashion by a dozen cows and four calves.

Surrounded by pines, this meadow bore tall grasses and bright flowers, all of them growing in sunlight filtered by needled boughs. A natural cathedral, he thought, this was a cloistered place that could have been reserved for worship. Was this his church? Birds sang like music from the angels, and butterflies fluttered by, drifting from one wildflower to another like stained glass windows come to life.

Howell's gaze swung left to right as he studied mountains visible through the treetops. Beyond hunger pangs now, he was weak. Water was plentiful in brooks coursing down the mountainsides. But he had no food. He had spotted small trout in streams, and nearly exhausted himself trying to catch one. Even if he succeeded, he realized he would have to eat the fish raw. He tried to eat an insect, but could not bring himself to put a crawling creature in his mouth. He ate grass. He found small red berries. A handful made him sick, and a day later his stomach still hurt from eating them.

Light-headed, Howell sank to his knees, not in prayer, but physically spent. Dropping to all fours, he stretched out in the cool and fragrant grass. He half turned and lay on his side, drawing his knees up. He could no longer deny the truth. First, he had lost the trail left by savages. Then he had lost his horse. Now he was lost. He knew he would not die of thirst in these forbidding mountains. A worse fate awaited. Death by starvation, he had once read in a seaman's account, came slowly and painfully, the final hours filled with mad delusions.

★ ★ ★

'Where . . . where are we going?'

Ella had not spoken to Seth until he stopped. They rested in cool shade cast by a massive spruce tree. She looked at his face, seeing irregular scars where the skin had been pulled together and sewn. It seemed to have been pieced like the hides of a teepee, and sewn to cover the socket where his left eye had been.

'A place the Cheyennes call Shadow Valley,' Seth replied.

'Shadow Valley,' she repeated. 'Where does that name come from?'

'The sun rises behind a mountain,' he said, 'and throws shadows against a cliff.' He glanced at her. 'Spirits of the

159

ancestors come up from the underworld and reveal their presence in shadows. That's what the old man chiefs say.'

She studied him. 'Where did you learn to speak English?' She saw him stiffen. He did not reply for a long moment.

'All Tribes School in Mintern, Wisconsin,' he said at last. 'I learned the white man's ways there.'

He stood abruptly and strode away. He halted between two spruce trees. Ella saw him kick away the cut boughs on the ground. She stared, unable to comprehend what he was doing.

Seth bent down. He picked up a bow and quiver of arrows that had been concealed there. Slinging the quiver over his shoulder, he picked up a pouch closed by a drawstring. When he came back, he offered her pemmican.

Ella accepted the food. She was amazed Seth had cached food and a weapon. He watched their back trail while he ate. Finished, he stood and motioned to her. She got to her feet and followed him into the forest.

Her mind was full of questions, but Seth was silent, avoiding her gaze. She understood his eagerness to put distance between them and the encampment. Judging from an annoyed glance back at her, he believed they were moving too slowly to make good their escape.

9

Peter Howell dreamed of crying, sobbing like a child separated from his parents. Then he imagined the sounds of a bell. Tinkling music seemed to come from a distance, but he knew the source was no farther away than a deep recess of his mind. Half-crazed by hunger, he covered his ears with his hands to block out one more weird hallucination, one more waking dream tormenting him.

He slowly lowered his hands, staring in disbelief as a belled donkey wandered into the meadow. Bearing packs, the mouse-gray creature trotted to him like a puppy expecting to be petted. The small brass bell around his neck tinkled delicately. Howell did not believe the animal or the bell to be real until a soft nose pressed against his chest.

Howell blinked. When he reached out to touch the animal, a man's rough voice came from behind him.

'Get yer god-damned hands off Becky Sue, mister.'

Startled, Howell spun around. He saw a thick-bodied, shaggy man dressed in a tattered coat, red flannel shirt, and patched trousers of blue wool. The man squinted over the sights of a long-barreled musket.

'Hands off my goods! Drop that 'ere gun. Drop it right now, or I'll blow yer god-damn' haid clean off.'

Howell shook in a sudden fit of shivering, as though taken with ague. In truth, he had never looked into the business end of a gun barrel before, and paralyzing fear surged through him. He heard the shaggy man let out a string of curses, again ordering him to drop the revolver under threat of death.

Fingers quivering, Howell tried to comply. He fumbled with the belt buckle. Amid growling curses from a man ready to kill him, he finally loosened his cartridge belt and let it fall to the ground with the holstered revolver.

'Who the hell are ye?'

'Peter . . . Peter Howell.'

'Well, Mister Peter Howell, what the hell ye doing in these parts? I heard ye caterwaulin' like a dying cat, so I moved in behind ye.' He looked him over. 'Afoot, are ye? Where's yer goods?'

'Gone,' Howell said meekly. 'All gone.'

'Ain't you some sorry sight.' He shook his head. 'If the god-damn' savages don't cut ye to pieces, by God, Lord Grizzly or Prince Cougar will chomp on ye fer supper.'

Howell eyed him. The man's bearded face was drawn, front teeth missing. Small, dark eyes peered through filthy hair sticking out under a sagging hat brim. His clothes were crudely patched, boots held together with wire. And he stank.

Howell fought off a wave of nausea as he stared at this man. He had seen his like in the Denver camp. Crawling with body lice and foul of voice, such men held a gun or knife at the ready day and night. They trusted no one. Most had committed horrendous crimes without

164

pangs of conscience, fearing only a back-shooter's revenge.

Howell drew a deep breath and let it out. Even though wracked by fear and weakened by hunger, he was not one to compromise his beliefs. He was ready to demand this foul-smelling man cease taking the Lord's name in vain, when his knees buckled. He fell heavily and rolled on his back. The last image in his mind was the face of Satan peering down at him — a scowling visage cast against the clear blue sky overhead.

His nostrils filled with the man's foul stench again when he was awakened by a hot liquid being poured down his throat. He coughed and came up on one elbow. He was aware of a smoky campfire in the meadow now, and some kind of broth being thrust at him in a dented cup. Howell faced the choice of drinking more, or having the contents poured down his throat.

'Hell, this ain't elk piss,' the shaggy man said. 'It's bone marrow in crick water, hot. Good fer what ails ye. Now, drink it.'

While the man tended the fire, Howell did as he was told. He lifted the cup to his mouth and drained it. He closed his eyes and rested. When he looked again, he shook himself, surprised to find the brew had revived him a bit.

'Sir, what is your name?'

'Zebulon Becker,' he replied. He knelt by the fire, peering into a blackened pan. 'I'm boiling some god-damn' venison. We'll eat as soon as it quits bleeding.'

'Thank you, Mister Becker . . . .'

Zebulon Becker cursed under his breath as wood smoke drifted into his eyes. Leaning back, he used his knife to stir the chunks of meat. Presently he brought several pieces to Howell in the empty cup, and then wielded the point of his knife to spear the meat out of the pan into his mouth, cursing all the while.

Howell ate with his fingers, gingerly handling the hot pieces of boiled meat. He saw Becker quickly finish. The man belched and vigorously rubbed his jaw with a grubby hand, complaining of pain in his teeth. He cast an impatient look at Howell.

'I done asked ye. Whatcha doing, wandering through these here god-damned mountains, afoot, by yer lonesome? Huh? Trying to get yerself killed?'

Howell fell silent. 'Mister Becker . . . .'

'Huh?'

'Mister Becker, I can see that you have fallen into the habit of taking the name of our Lord in vain.'

Zebulon Becker eyed him, one bushy eyebrow cocked. 'What're ye driving at?'

'I would appreciate it, sir,' Howell said, 'if you ceased that cursing.'

'Oh, ye would, would ye?' Becker demanded.

'Bow your head in prayer, sir,' Howell said, 'and speak reverently of our God Almighty.'

'Well, hell's fire, I'd appreciate it,' Becker said in a mocking voice, 'if ye ceased calling call me 'sir.''

'I beg your pardon?'

'Ye don't have to beg nothing,' Becker said. He waved at the pan. 'Speaking of which. Ye warn't too proud to et my supper, was ye? Ye sure as hell can take venison off me. And ye never lifted a finger to get that fire up, did ye?'

Howell met his stare, and changed the subject. 'In answer to your question, Mister Becker . . . .'

'Ye can stop calling me 'mister,' too,' he broke in. 'Don't put on no airs. Jest say what ye mean, straight out.' He added in a taunt: 'God dammit.'

Howell drew another deep breath. Then he answered Becker's question, briefly recounting events that brought him here. He saw keen interest light up the man's eyes.

'Hold on. Yer huntin' a girl stoled by savages?'

Howell nodded.

'What's her name?'

'Ella Mae Campbell.'

Becker eyed him. 'What's she look like?'

Howell described her as best he could, at once feeling a chill run up his back. Becker's sudden interest revealed the

168

truth. He had seen her. Howell felt certain of that.

'Where is she, Mister Becker?'

'Now, didn't I jest tell ye to cease putting on airs?'

Jaw clenched, Howell nodded once. Despite appearances, this man possessed a shrewd intelligence. Howell repeated his question, leaving out the mister: 'Where is she?'

'People of the Blue Lake got her,' Becker replied.

'Who?'

Zebulon Becker waved toward the distant mountain peaks streaked with snow. 'Cheyenne and Arapaho clans camped over yonder on the shore of a lake . . . a hunnert lodges. People of the Blue Lake. That's what they call theirselves.'

★ ★ ★

Ella struggled to match the pace set by Seth. She sweated under the buckskin dress as she followed him through forested valleys and over rocky, bare ridges

169

beyond the blue lake. She could not keep up with his easy stride, and he frequently stopped, barely concealing his impatience while waiting for her to catch up.

More than time to catch up, she needed rest, a few minutes to fill her lungs at this altitude, a few more minutes to nurse feet sore from sharp rocks in the trail. Her moccasins afforded some protection, but not as much as the sturdy shoes she was accustomed to wearing.

At his silent urging, she pressed on, grimacing, but without complaint. Several times that morning Seth plunged downslope to rushing water. Ella followed as they waded in brooks, leaving no trail for pursuers to follow.

After noon, that first day, they reached another cache of food. This one was placed under rocks stacked on the steep slope of a ridge. While eating, Seth again studied their back trail.

'Are they following us?' she whispered.

He shrugged. 'Bow Strings know where to find me.'

'Then why are we hiding our tracks?'

'Call it pride.'

She did not understand that answer. Another, more urgent, question came to her mind: 'Will that warrior, Eagle Feather, come after me?'

Seth looked at her. 'You ask plenty of questions.'

'Will he?'

'Don't worry,' Seth replied. 'I'll take you to your people.'

'But . . . but won't the warriors kill you,' she asked, 'if they catch us?'

He chewed dried meat, jaw moving slowly, as though considering his answer. He said nothing. Swallowing, he stood and motioned for her to follow him. They set out again.

For the remainder of that day and two more days, they made their way through cañons and over low, rocky mountains. Clearly Seth knew the way. He moved with confidence from one food cache to the next. He rarely spoke. Silent observation was his way. He often paused on high ground, as motionless as a deer while watching their back trail. Nights they slept side by side deep in forests. The first night Ella sat up for hours, fighting off sleep until she dozed. She did not know if she could trust Seth. Groggy, she realized she had to trust him. Her only choice was to return to the Cheyenne encampment — if she could find it.

From then on she slept with her back to him, and he did not touch her. She asked questions, but when he answered only with a nod or shake of his head, she grew silent, too. His attention was still focused on their back trail, and in the hours before nightfall he frequently left her to scout for pursuing warriors.

She gradually understood the depth of his plan, the methodical care and thought that had gone into it, and knew why he had not freed her sooner. First he'd had to lay out food on the route. Then he had waited for a moonless night. His planning had led to a swift escape from a well-guarded encampment, and now they traveled safely with his promise to return her to her people.

On the third day the sun was low in the western sky when they reached an overlook. Ella caught up with Seth, and moved to his side. She stared into the long valley opening before them, struck silent by the sight of a great rift in the mountainous terrain. It was dizzying, for the gorge was more than a thousand feet deep and ten or twelve miles in width. Native grasses covered much of the open valley floor; the rest was densely forested.

The great valley was flanked by gray cliffs and towering spires of stone on the summit of a far ridge. Below, Ella spotted a creek meandering through the high grass. The serpentine waterway was marked by a string of beaver ponds, each golden pool reflecting the fading light of an evening sky. When Seth did not move on, Ella looked at him questioningly.

'This is it,' he said, for once answering an unasked question. 'Shadow Valley.'

She gazed into the deep gorge until Seth began his descent. Footsore, she walked gingerly behind him. She asked: 'Where are the spirits?'

'More questions,' he said over his shoulder.

'I may learn to believe in spirits,' she said, 'if you tell me where to look for them.'

Ella glimpsed a smile crossing his lips — another first. He halted, standing on a flat expanse of stone that overlooked the great valley. He pointed due west, directing her gaze to sheer walls of granite. Then his arm swung toward the towering stone formations on the summit of the ridge to the east.

'The sun comes up behind those spires,' he said, 'casting shadows across the valley to the cliffs over there. Indian people believe the shadows reveal spirits. Sacred spirits appear with each phase of the moon, rising up from the underworld to protect them. Or warn of danger.'

'What kind of danger?'

'All kinds,' he replied. 'Weather, sickness, Ute warriors.' He added: 'Strangers.'

'Is that what I am to them?'

He glanced at her. 'The women of the tribe say you walk with the spirit of a poisonous snake. No one is safe in your presence.'

Ella told him about the gold watch in the possession of Eagle Feather. 'He killed my father. Didn't he?'

Seth said nothing. If he knew of her father's fate, his stoic expression gave no hint of it.

Ella studied him in profile. Seth was a puzzle. His face was a rich earthen color, his chin bold, cheek bones high and sharp, his one-eyed gaze intense. She looked at the patchwork of scars where the skin had been pulled together and stitched like a quilt to cover his eye socket. She wanted to ask how the injury had befallen him, but he turned and strode away.

Ella followed as he moved downslope on a game trail littered with elk and deer droppings. The trail wound through downed timber, bare-limbed pines tangled after toppling in a rockslide. They made their way through skeletal trees and over boulders to the bottom. A stream meandered through willows and long blades of green grass.

Ella followed Seth as he waded into the clear water bubbling over rounded stones. The water eddied, swirled, and flowed onward, a timeless force of nature. Cupping ice-cold water in their hands, they drank quickly and moved on.

Tired, she staggered. She forced herself to place one sore foot in front of the other, legs weak as she marshaled all of her determination. She knew she could not go much farther. Fortunately she did not have to. Ahead, thick, white-barked aspen trees surrounded a break in the forest. Seth led her to a fire ring there. Ella dropped to her knees near the blackened stones in the burned circle.

She saw Seth stride to the far side of the clearing. He disappeared in the evening shadows cast by the trees. Presently he came back with a rucksack slung over his shoulder.

Seth knelt beside her. He opened the pack, bringing out more dried meat. Ella knew she should eat, but her eyes closed. She stretched out. Lying in cool and fragrant grass in this protected place, she fell asleep.

* * *

Peter Howell should have guessed what was coming, but, when he heard Zebulon Becker set the conditions of Ella Mae Campbell's rescue, he was more than offended. He was outraged. It was nothing short of outrageous for any man to profit from tragic circumstances, much less for this stinking reprobate to make money from Ella Mae's captivity.

'The girl, she told me her pa was a man of means, as they say. Said he works fer some tradin' company back East. Said five hunnert dollars was fair. What do ye say to that?'

Howell stared at the leaping flames of the campfire.

'It's only fair to make it worth my while,' Becker insisted. 'If I guide a passel of white men with guns to that blue lake, I won't get no more trading out of them stinking bastards.' He shook his head slowly. 'The savages, they'll slit my god-damned throat if they get half a chance.'

Howell held his tongue. He knew if he spoke his mind, he would only alienate Becker. Better to string the conniving trader along, for now. He did not know what would happen when Becker learned Earl Campbell had not survived the attack by savages, but this was not the time to worry about that. Howell needed a guide out of these mountains. He had to get back to the Denver camp as soon as possible.

'I'll take two hunnert and fifty in gold from her pa,' Becker went on, 'and then he forks over the rest when we bring her out.' He paused, eyeing Howell. 'Do we have us a deal, or don't we?'

Howell looked up from red-yellow flames, blinking rapidly as though he had been staring into the depths of hell. 'We have a deal, Mister Becker.'

So be it, Howell thought, sanctifying a lie for the purpose of deceiving Satan himself.

Awakened by the sun full on her, Ella felt warmth seeping through her buckskin dress. The radiant heat felt good on her body. She rolled over, seeking more. Exhausted last night, she had scarcely moved after stretching out in the grass. Now she sat up. She looked around. Seth was not in sight.

Grimacing, she got to her feet. She was sore from the length of her thighs to the bottoms of her feet. Every motion brought pain. Yet she knew she had to move around to loosen her stiff muscles. Making her way to the creek, she knelt and drank the cold water. A deep pool eddied here. She unbraided her hair, bent over the creek, and tried to wash out the grease that had been applied by the crone. The position was awkward and painful.

Ella looked around. She scanned the white-barked trees encircling this campsite. Satisfied she was alone, she slipped out of her dress. She waded into the pool

179

to her waist and then to shoulder depth, the cold water raising goose-bumps on her bare skin. Submerging herself, she scrubbed her hair with a vigorous rubbing of both hands. She came up for air, gasping.

Ella forced herself to do it again, and then a third dunking. She stayed in the icy water as long as she could bear it. Numbed, she stepped out of the water into the grass. She dropped to her knees and stretched out, using her buckskin dress for a pallet. Her bare skin was warmed by the sun. She felt refreshed — and hungry. She rested for a time, and pulled on her dress. Her legs were still sore, but her hair was clean for the first time in a long while.

Moving closer to the fire ring, she opened Seth's rucksack and rummaged through it. It was sturdy, made from leather stitched to heavy canvas. She found a label under the flap: **All Tribes School, Mintern, Wisconsin.**

Along with a thin-bladed skinning knife, arrowheads, sinew, and flint, she found jerky and pemmican in the rucksack. This time she ate the dried food in gulping mouthfuls, soon returning to the creek. She drank again. Rippling waters masked sounds. When she raised up from water's edge, she turned, surprised to see Seth stride into the meadow. He halted at the fire ring.

He bent over the circle of blackened stones, striking flint. Wisps of smoke drifted up from a pile of dry twigs and leaves. He gently blew into it. Small flames came to life. He fed them with larger sticks, building a fire.

She watched as he fashioned a cooking paunch from the lining of an elk's stomach. His supply of fresh meat, he explained, was hidden in a cave a short distance away. The cave was cool, and the mouth of it was blocked off by stones to make a bear-proof cache.

Suspended from a willow tripod over the flames, Seth used hot stones to heat the fresh meat and vegetables inside the paunch. Through the morning, wild peas, turnips, and elk meat cooked into a pungent stew — ready to eat before noon. The next day, when the paunch was softened by the heat of embers outside and hot stones inside, they would eat it, too.

Refreshed, Ella stole glances at Seth. He rarely looked directly at her. When his one-eyed gaze lifted to meet hers, no words were spoken, but a certain communication passed between them. They both knew the time had come. In the morning they would leave Shadow Valley.

'Seth.'

He gazed at her.

'How long did you go to the All Tribes School?' she asked.

'Too long,' he replied.

'What do you mean by that?' she asked. When he offered no reply other than a shrug, she added recklessly: 'I always loved school. Even after we moved to Baltimore where I had no friends, I loved my teachers . . . .'

He gazed at her. 'How much would you have loved school if you were sent to a foreign land where you were punished every time you spoke or even whispered words of your language?'

'Punished?' Ella repeated in surprise.

'My mouth was washed out with soap,' he went on, 'the first few times I was caught saying Cheyenne words. Then I was caned for disobedience and put in a small room called The Box. I was allowed to come out after I had promised to speak my language no more. A friend and I ran away.'

Ella stared in amazement.

'We were caught in a farmer's field,' Seth went on. 'My friend was whipped like a bad dog. When I tried to get away, I tripped and fell against the farmer's plow. The blade slashed my face and cut into my left eye.'

'Oh, Seth,' Ella said.

He shrugged again. 'It was an accident. No one meant to blind me in one eye. The Carter family at the school had always been good to me. They gave me a new name because they thought I could be squeezed and shaped into a white child.' He paused. 'I ran away again, by myself. No one came after me. I think they were glad for me to be gone so they would not have to look at me every day and be reminded of their cruelty.'

Ella lowered her gaze. This account was the most she had ever heard Seth speak, and now, instead of carrying on a long conversation, she was silenced by the impact of his words.

That night, without a word exchanged between them, they came together, embraced, and slept in one another's arms beside the glowing embers of the campfire.

At dawn Seth leaped to his feet. Ella raised up. She looked around in the dim light of morning. Men stood perfectly still in the shadows of the aspen trees surrounding this meadow on three sides.

Eagle Feather stepped forward, bow and arrow in hand. Many Bears and the other Bow String warriors closed in, all of them armed and painted for combat.

10

The poet, Dante, could not have conjured up a fate worse than this. Peter Howell reached that conclusion while walking behind a farting donkey beside a yammering jackass. Zebulon Becker was a man who could not refrain from talking. After a time, his mindless cursing was the least of it. This man uttered endless complaints, shouted horrific threats against anyone who had ever wronged him, and repeated himself in an unending litany of condemnations. His clamorous voice demanded attention, yet the sheer volume of it drowned out any comment from Howell. Even asleep, the torment continued with the gap-toothed mouth wide open while Becker snored to the heavens. This sawing was interrupted by the occasional explosion of coughing when a night insect was sucked into the foul opening.

The booming voice of the trader

resounded through cañons and across the land as they followed creeks winding out of the mountains to the lower foothills. The air turned hot where the foothills rolled out to the great, colorless prairie. Howell had lost track of time, but the day came when he spotted a smear of smoke on the horizon ahead, due west — the Denver camp. Becky Sue must have caught wind of it, too, for she picked up the pace.

Becker swore as he hauled back on the donkey's lead rope. He peered ahead. He claimed the camp teemed with cheats and killers. After one final demand, he shut his mouth at last.

'Remember our deal. Five hunnert, gold. Which ain't a fair shake fer me. Hell, no. I won't be able to trade with them bastards no more. Give the savages half a chance, and they'll slit my god-damn' throat.'

Howell had heard it a hundred times. Becker peeled off when they drew near the camp. With Becky Sue's bell tinkling, the trader headed for a deadfall where he claimed he was owed drinks in exchange for a white fox pelt traded there last season.

Howell offered no word of parting or gratitude to his guide. He simply turned away from this foul man and strode toward his campsite across the South Platte River. He had been gone for a matter of weeks, the exact number he did not know, but his time in the wilderness felt like eternity.

He had been gone long enough, he discovered, for rumors of his demise to have taken on currency. His wife and daughter stared as he waded the shallow river, lifting his arms in a ghost-like pose. Shocked silence turned to shouts of joy and shrill squeals as Jane and Christina came running to him, water splashing with each leaping stride. They crashed into his arms, nearly knocking him down. Howell embraced his wife and daughter midstream, tearful and mute, at last delivered from his misery.

Others ventured to the riverbank, settlers pointing at Howell and turning to one another while repeating news of their discovery. The loudest voice came from the biggest man, Jake Osborne.

'Alive! Howell's alive! He's alive!'

The widow Gustafson stood with her clinging children, her expression stoic. All five Osbornes ran around, jumping like coyote pups, and shouted as they became caught up in the excitement of the moment. Missing was Millicent Campbell.

Crossing the river, arm in arm, with his wife and daughter, Howell answered their urgent question: 'Ella Mae is alive.'

'Where is she?'

'Is she all right?'

'Have they hurt her?'

To the settlers and placer miners who gathered around him, Howell found himself regarded as a hero. He had survived the ordeal, alone until he had hooked up with the trader, Zebulon Becker.

Howell did not mention the man's demand for compensation, and admitted he had not actually seen Ella Mae or the lodge where she was held prisoner.

But Becker knew, and Becker would take them to the blue lake. Howell made this promise behind Becker's back, knowing full well the man would learn of Earl Campbell's death sooner or later. There would be no payment of five cents, much less five hundred dollars. But if the trader were expected by good folks to guide a rescue party, Howell figured public pressure would force him to do the right thing.

By the light of a campfire, Howell revealed his plan for rescuing Ella Mae. A group of armed volunteers would mount a charge into the encampment. Taking his authority from the frontiersman, Buell Harris, he stated firearms were known to frighten the savages. With a fierce charge, muskets and pistols blazing, Howell was confident the savages would be driven from their lodges. Even if they only fled out of musket range, that margin would allow enough time to locate Ella Mae, free her, and beat a hasty retreat out of the mountains.

Listeners were inspired by this plan.

Leaping to their feet, several men claimed they could be ready to leave at dawn. Howell thanked the volunteers, but begged for rest. He retired that night a hero.

He was not surprised to find that his wife and daughter had accomplished a great deal in his absence. Jane was a hard worker, and Christina was expected to do her share, too. The garden was in, and a tent had been constructed from discards.

'We had to busy ourselves,' Jane explained to her husband that night as they lay side by side on a thin mattress, 'to keep from losing our minds to worry. Chrissy and I shed tears every night when we prayed for your safety. I confess our hopes flagged. After all we've been through since the death of Earl Campbell . . . well, the thought of never seeing you again was more than we could bear.'

With the help of Osborne, Jane and Christina had acquired extra side boards and top bows from abandoned wagons. Using weathered canvas wagon covers, they had pieced together a tent of sorts on the Howell claim, a patch of ground at the base of the bluff where Sunday services were held.

The tent was livable for now, sheltering the inhabitants from the sudden afternoon rainstorms and sharp, swirling winds that spiraled dust into the air in this desolate part of the world. For survival through the winter, a more substantial structure would be built. A second sawmill had been shipped disassembled, this one steam-powered, and would arrive in freight outfits. Demand for lumber was high, and a site for the new saw had been selected. Men had been hired to fell trees and drag in logs from the mountain forests.

'Where is she?' Howell asked.

'Millie?'

'Yes.'

'In her wagon,' Jane replied. 'She rarely comes out.' She rested her hand on his chest and whispered: 'Peter, I think she is determined to die.'

After sunup Howell went to the

Campbell wagon. 'Millie. Millie, it's me . . . Peter.'

He spoke her name again before pulling open the wagon cover to peer inside. A stench of body odor and urine wafted into his nostrils. In the canvas-filtered light he saw the frail figure lying on dirty blankets inside. Millicent did not move, and for a moment he believed she had passed on. Then her head turned, her deep-set eyes finding him.

Howell spoke softly, telling her about Ella Mae and his plan for rescuing her. The words seemed to have no more meaning than prairie winds, and her eyes closed. Howell withdrew.

Over a breakfast of oatmeal, sausage, and hot tea, Jane and Christina brought him up to date on various events that had transpired during his absence: rumors of gold strikes in mountain gulches were rampant, nearly always unproven; one of the Osborne children had survived a rattlesnake bite; several families from the Brethren Wagon Company had located water a few miles south of the

Denver camp, and had staked claims; steel-bladed plows now plied the land, cutting sod untouched through the eons; crops had been planted in time for an autumn harvest; an altercation near cribs occupied by prostitutes had left a dozen men injured and four others mortally wounded, a running fight that resulted in pleas for troops to keep order in a lawless camp; as proof of the lawlessness, the body of Bernard Cleeve had been found in a thicket by the river. Throat slit, the teamster had been robbed of his boots, pistol, and money belt.

★　★　★

Ella stared at the silent warriors. They eased out of the shadows cast by the trees, slowly converging on them, bows raised. Seth made no move toward his bow and arrow or the bone-handled knife sheathed on his belt. He stared at the warriors, his scarred face showing no fear.

Ella was struck by the hopelessness

of this moment. If these warriors meant to kill them, no force short of an earthquake could stop them. Eagle Feather spoke.

Seth listened, and replied. The tall warrior's dark-eyed gaze swept past Ella as though he had no interest in her. She sensed he did, though, and then she asked Seth what was being said.

'Eagle Feather says I stole you from him,' he replied. 'He thinks the Ute squaw helped me. Now he wants horses in payment.'

She stared. 'Payment? For me?'

'He traded horses for you. Now he wants horses.'

'What . . . what are you going to do?'

'Nothing.'

'Nothing!'

He glanced at her. 'Eagle Feather knows I don't own any horses. So do these Bow Strings. They all know Eagle Feather is rich with horses.'

'Then why is he making such a demand?'

Seth glanced at her. 'You ask too many

questions.'

'My life is at stake,' she said. 'I have a right to know what's going on.'

Seth considered that notion, and shrugged. 'When a wealthy man dismisses a debt, he proves he's the better man. Eagle Feather just now proved this in front of warriors who respect him.'

'But . . . but what's going to happen?' Ella asked.

Seth ignored her question, but after another exchange with Eagle Feather he turned to her. 'He says the spirits of Shadow Valley appeared this morning. One took the form of a snake from the underworld. Remember the old man chief who purified you with ashes? He says you have powers awarded by a snake. Now Eagle Feather wants you to hear him.'

'Hear him?' she repeated. 'I don't understand.'

'Stop asking questions long enough to listen,' he said, 'and maybe you will understand.'

She cast an angry look at him, but,

when the men put down their weapons and gathered around the campfire, she did as he suggested. Eagle Feather spoke first. His voice was deep and resonant, his hand gestures graceful. She listened to Seth's translation of his words, beginning with 'the time when we lost the corn.'

Their grandfathers, Eagle Feather said, and all of the grandfathers before them hunted and farmed and fished in the region known to whites as Minnesota and western Wisconsin. Attacked by white men with guns, they were forced to leave their lands for a life of hunting on the Great Plains. They followed buffalo herds migrating with the seasons. With horses and secure lodges transported by travois, the hunting life had met the needs of the People. Under the protection of their warrior societies, they prospered.

But the advance of the white tribes was relentless. Eagle Feather remembered how his father had watched darkening prairie skies with foreboding. Lightning flashes in black clouds signified guns of the white men, he believed. They were coming.

In the autumn moon, Eagle Feather remembered from childhood the last hunt of the season had been successful. Hunters of the Bear Paw clan had downed five buffaloes, and women and children had easily caught up with them. Carcasses were skinned, the heavy hides stretched out with pegs driven into the ground. Scraped, the hides would be softened and made pliable, useful to the People for clothing or bedding. Buffalo meat was cut and sliced into thin strips. Sun-dried food for the coming winter represented the margin between survival and starvation.

In that autumn moon scouts spotted a rising plume of dust on the horizon, and whistled a warning. The people of the Bear Paw clan backed away as seven mounted strangers materialized under the cloud of dust. Bearded white men came galloping across the plains, all of them armed with long-barreled buffalo guns. They began firing from a great distance, shooting warriors armed with bows and arrows. Well-mounted, the whites ran down fleeing women and children, killing most of them outright with handguns while leaving others on the ground, bleeding from mortal wounds.

The boy, shot in the back, did not die. Trailing blood, he crawled into a ravine and lay behind a clump of flowering rabbitbrush. He heard horses and rough voices. After nightfall the moon came up, and a vast silence lay upon the land like an unknown spirit. The boy heard no more moaning, no more cries, and crawled out of the ravine.

By the light of the full moon he saw the bodies. All were dead. His grandfather. His grandmother. His father. His mother. His two brothers and four young sisters. Six Bear Paw warriors. Scalped, they lay still on the moonlit plain. The five buffalo hides were gone.

For the rest of his life, the boy would mourn the murder of his family. And he wondered why buffalo meat had been left to rot. As a youth and later as a man, he understood the whites were murderous, that they killed without provocation, but he could not understand why anyone would leave meat to rot.

The next day this boy was found by Bear Paw relatives who had heard the shooting, and concealed themselves. His rescuers saw a rattlesnake slither away. It was known to the People that spirits sometimes made themselves visible through animals, and this serpent was believed to have meaning for the boy. The story stayed with him, even after he had earned his adult name.

Seth paused. In the silence that followed, Eagle Feather turned his back to Ella. He showed her the dimple under his shoulder blade, a scar left by a bullet fired at long range from a buffalo gun. The bullet was still lodged in his body.

Eagle Feather had taken particular notice of her, Seth explained, when she had survived the snakebite. He did not want her as a wife or even as a slave like the old Ute woman who had cared for

Ella. He wanted only to know her feminine powers, to understand the link between that spirit and his life now as a leader of warriors in the Bow String Society.

After translating his words, Seth turned and spoke to Eagle Feather. A silence followed. For the first time the warrior looked squarely at Ella.

'What was said?' she asked.

'I told him about your father,' Seth replied. He paused. 'And I told him about the gold watch.'

* * *

Under a blistering hot sun Howell withstood a blistering hot cursing from Zebulon Becker. Enraged, the trader's profane words tumbled from his gap-toothed mouth like hot rocks. Howell's silence, a studied refusal to reply in kind, angered the man even more.

From a saloon man named Aaron Cahill, Becker had learned the details of the attack on the Brethren Wagon

Company. The fight was still a subject of discussion in the Denver camp. Among the dead was Earl Campbell, father of the girl who was taken by savages. Discovering this, Becker stormed after Howell, found him, and heaped curses upon him. He was silenced only when Jake Osborne intervened.

'Don't talk to our preacher that way,' he said.

Becker turned his rage on the big man. 'Ye call him a preacher? A God-fearing man? Hell, he's nothing but a lying bastard . . . .'

Osborne raised a beefy fist and moved a step closer. 'I done told you. Shut your mouth. Shut it, if you don't wanna lose what few teeth you got left in that hairy hole.'

Becker glowered at him. 'Mister, I could take offense at them words.'

'You do that.'

Drool trickled out of the corner of Becker's mouth, a foaming stream lost in his unkempt beard. He turned and walked away, shouting one last blast over his shoulder.

'I ain't a-gonna guide no god-damn' rescue party to the Blue Lake. Not now, god damn ye, not ever!'

Howell discovered the threat was not idle. That day Becker made the rounds, spreading the word to all who would listen that an attack on the savages would be costly. First, the distance was great, the trek arduous under a hot sun; second, the mountainous terrain beyond the prairie was ill-suited for travel on horseback; third, Bow String warriors, alert for raiding Utes, would quickly detect the presence of white men tramping through the forest. Becker described a busy encampment of 'two hunnert, maybe three hunnert' lodges backing up to the lake, well guarded by warriors who would make short work of settlers charging into the clearing, guns or no guns.

Peter Howell had known Becker possessed a shrewd intelligence, and he reconfirmed this fact when he sought settlers and placer miners willing to ride with him. Becker had single-handedly turned the camp against him. In addition to perils, Becker had convinced anyone who would listen that Ella was not in immediate danger. By now she had already been 'ruined,' he said, from repeated rapes. After tribesmen were finished with her, she would be either be taken as a slave, or banished from the camp by stone-throwing women of the tribe.

In his rôle as trader with the Indians, Becker offered to facilitate Ella's release himself. All he needed were trade articles. Goods donated by the men and women of the Denver camp just might make enough of a swap for him to bring her out, easy as pie.

Howell's jaw clenched when he learned of this. Becker's capacity for chicanery could hardly be underestimated. Howell wondered how he could be the only man in the Denver camp who saw through the schemes of a thief. If Becker succeeded in taking up a collection in the name of Ella Mae Campbell, the man would keep the proceeds for himself.

On the raw frontier, Howell learned, laws were fluid at best, enforced haphazardly. Settlers were often ruled by bullies, cheated by liars. Howell also learned most folks believed what they wanted to believe. First, they had responded to his urgent call for a rescue party. But now the words of an Indian trader persuaded them to reconsider. A trek deep into unmapped mountain gorges was not the stuff of a heroic ride, but merely a fool's venture resulting in torture and death at the hands of brutal savages. As proof, Becker had pointed out, hadn't Howell himself fled when he was led out of the maze of twisting cañons?

Howell tried to counter the argument, but few settlers or miners sided with him now. Levi Case and Aaron Cahill were no different. Howell found the two men after he had spotted the Case boys lounging in hot shade outside the saloon owned by Cahill. The brothers were taking turns throwing a Bowie knife into a log, the long blade flashing end over end before sticking deeply in the wood.

Howell shook hands with Jared and Jason. After inviting them to Sunday services, he entered a saloon reeking of soggy chaw, stale tobacco smoke, and spilled liquor.

'Preacher Howell!'

He heard the commanding voice of Levi Case, and made his way through the dark shadows to a round gaming table near the rear wall, the same one where he had found them last time he had come here. This time Case did not invite him to sit down.

'I hear tell,' Case said, 'that you still aim to raise a militia to hunt down the savages.'

Howell stood by the table. 'Can I count on you?'

'Yes, sir, you certainly may.'

The easy rejoinder caught Howell off guard.

'Yes sir,' Case repeated with a laugh. 'You may count on me to use common sense.'

'I beg your pardon?'

'Any man who blunders into mountain cañons crawling with savages will not come out alive,' Case said with a laugh. 'That is what common sense tells me.'

Peter Howell eyed him, recalling a promise Case had made when blood had been spilled in the savages' attack on the settlers' campsite. He had not expected aid from Levi Case now, but he resented his cavalier attitude, empty words from a self-described gentleman who used lofty verbiage to cover the truth.

Howell announced a proposal he had been considering ever since he figured out Zebulon Becker had outmaneuvered him. 'It would appear that I have no other choice but to pass a petition through the camp.'

'Petition,' Case repeated. 'What kind of petition?'

'An emergency request for a company of troops to rescue Ella Mae Campbell from the savages,' Howell said. 'Most folks will sign it. Troopers have already been requested for law enforcement. I believe the territorial governor will act on it quickly.'

Levi Case stiffened. 'Yankee bluecoats aren't needed in this territory, Preacher. You know that as well as I do.'

'No, I don't believe I do,' Howell countered in a flippant rejoinder of his own.

Levi Case studied him. 'If you aim to bring the war out here to the territories, Preacher Howell, that's the way to do it.'

'Mister Case,' Howell said, mocking the man's formality, 'all of us walk on federal land. You intend to profit from it, don't you? Fact is the United States Army is empowered to enforce laws and protect the citizenry . . . unless you aim to fence your ranch and secede.'

Case slammed a hand down on the table and stood, glowering. Aaron Cahill got to his feet, too.

'Sir,' the saloon man said, 'you are no longer welcome here.'

Howell eyed both men long enough to let them know he was not cowed, and left. Outside, in glaring sunlight, the two teen-aged boys were still throwing the knife, the blade sticking in wood with a dull *thunk*. Howell bid them good bye as he turned and headed for his camp.

Sunday morning dawned bright and sunny. At ten, Peter Howell met the gazes of the gathered worshippers, his voice strong with passion as he read from the book of Psalms: "Thou preparest a table before me in the presence of mine enemies . . . goodness and mercy shall follow me all the days of my life . . . I will dwell in the house of the Lord. For eternity."

He counted heads while leading his congregation in prayer, not to calculate tithes as cynics claimed preachers routinely did, but to determine if enough men were present to haul stone and to stack logs for the construction of a church on the crest of this bluff.

Howell needed a work force now, not gunmen. Through prayer, he had come to terms with his failure to raise a militia. He had drawn up a petition requesting a company of troopers, and passed it. As he expected, there was no shortage of men eager to sign. The petition became a loyalty oath of sorts. Southern sympathizers declined, seeing this request as another act of war from a tyrannical federal government.

Now the faces of forty-two worshippers were shaded by wide-brimmed hats, sunbonnets, and parasols, their voices rising and falling as they sang hymns under the direction of Jane and Christina. The music of their voices washed over Howell, bringing a familiar peace to his soul. This pleasurable moment was interrupted by ear-piercing shrieks. Howell realized the sounds came from the direction of his campsite.

He moved to the edge of the bluff and looked down the slope, amazed to see Millicent Campbell standing there. Hatless, her tattered dress hung from her emaciated body, a twig-like arm pointing to the far bank of the South Platte River. Her distressed calls turned to thin bleats, sounds reminding Howell of a dying rabbit.

Her mind has snapped, he thought,

until he looked across the river where she pointed. A lone figure slowly crossed the muddy bank and approached the water. At that moment he understood the cries of a mother for her child: 'Ella Mae! Ella Mae! Ella Mae!'

Part Two

Part Two

11

Colorado Territory
July, 1861

Ella Mae Campbell knelt beside two
graves on the bluff overlooking Denver.
The camp was becoming a town with a
grid of new streets and new frame buildings on stone foundations. A church built
on this hill, as she had heard Preacher
Howell tell his congregation, would
signal another important step in the
transition from a littered mining camp
reeking of human waste and rotting garbage to a town with a measure of order
and services. Family men had been too
busy constructing their own dwellings to
build a church, but no one doubted it
would come to pass, someday.

Ella carried a handful of prairie sun-
flowers, the green leaves already wilting
in mid-summer heat, and gazed at two
wooden markers side by side. As a child,
she had believed all cemeteries were old,

213

old and shaded by great, dark trees. Back East, she remembered seeing gray stone markers overgrown with vines, moss obscuring names and dates recorded long before her birth. A cemetery was dark and vaguely forbidding, holding no meaning for her. Even her grandmother's death was but a distant memory, solemn impressions overshadowed by her mother's relentless grieving.

On the frontier, though, every aspect of life was new — death included. The graves on the bluff where Peter Howell had declared the First Brethren Church would stand one day were new and fraught with meaning for Ella. Vivid memories of her father and mother — their faces, their expressions, their gestures — were fresh in her mind.

She brought prairie flowers every week to the carved plank ends marking two graves:

Millicent Smith Campbell
b. Jan. 23, 1819
d. September 25, 1860

Earl Rory Campbell
b. April 11, 1817
d. July 2, 1860

She had watched her mother die. All these months later she was still haunted by it, baffled and frustrated by her own helplessness. She no longer wept, but she still grieved. At times she resented her mother, for it had seemed death had been summoned, an act of will that had left Ella here, alone.

Everyone who had known Millicent from the Brethren Wagon Company had believed she would 'perk up' in the weeks after she had been reunited with her daughter. But the frail woman did not perk up, even though spoon-fed corn meal mush and goat's milk by a loving daughter who bathed her and spoke tenderly to her, and sang softly as one would comfort a sick child. Millicent simply wasted away, bloodshot eyes closing, and drew her last breath.

Ella searched her mind for an explanation, a reason. Months later, the question still would not leave her inner-most thoughts.

From Peter and Jane Howell, Ella learned of her mother's state of mind after the attack on the wagon train. In answer to her questions, the preacher and his wife offered a theory: for too long Millicent had been a woman lost to life. By the time Ella returned, she was gaunt, pained by bedsores, and it was too late to reverse death's march. The day came when she slipped away, dying in her sleep as though fulfilling a promise to join her husband for eternity.

The funeral service had been held on the top of the bluff near stones that had been carried in and positioned roughly to mark the foundation of a church. In his graveside service, Peter Howell had recounted his first meeting with the Campbell family. It had occurred in July of '60, he had said, on the east bank of the Mississippi River. He described a mad jumping-off place crowded with pioneers-to-be, their Conestoga wagons and oxen, livestock ranging from hens to horses, mules to goats, in all a great cacophony of the voices of man and beast.

Howell had gone on to characterize their westward trek as 'a forge welding a great and strong friendship between two families.' The murder of Earl Campbell and kidnapping of Ella Mae, Howell had said to gathered mourners, cleaved the spirit of a loving wife and devoted mother. With her death, he had concluded, the savages had taken another innocent life.

In private moments, Ella reviewed the catastrophic events in her life — the death of her mother, the murder of her father, and the gold watch stolen from his pocket as he lay dead. She tried to reconcile herself to the fact that she might never find answers to her haunting questions. She believed she had some purpose for being here. Now she yearned to find her place, whether it was here on the frontier or back home, and escape the twin heartaches of helplessness and hopelessness.

Over the winter Jake Osborne had achieved that goal. He was not trapped by the past. A teetotaler now, he was a man changed in more ways than one. He had at last found a measure of peace in his life when he had moved Clara's remains from the prairie gravesite to the new cemetery on the barren crest of the bluff. In the same journey, he had exhumed the body of Earl Campbell. He laid him to rest beside Millicent's grave in the cemetery. Then he brought discarded plank ends from the new sawmill, and laboriously shaped and chiseled markers for all three graves.

Instead of returning to Indiana in the spring, Jake Osborne had stayed in the Denver camp. He had good reason. With nine children and many friends from the original Brethren Wagon Company looking on one fine Sunday afternoon, he had married Greta Gustafson. She had beamed during a wedding service she well understood without knowing more than a dozen words of English. In answer to the time-honored question, he had said — 'Yeah.' — and she shouted — 'Jah!' — and for the first time in memory the woman smiled when Peter Howell pronounced them husband and wife.

★ ★ ★

'Did they hurt you?'

The question echoed through the camp. Whether asked outright by Christina or whispered behind the hands of settler women, Ella could not escape it. Months later, wherever she went in Denver, stares followed. So did whispered remarks and cruel comments.

Men, whether drinking in saloons or whittling in liveries, agreed with solemn nods of authority that a woman raped by savages is forever ruined. Women in sewing circles and reading groups marked calendars. They predicted Ella would give birth to a half-breed child within nine months of her capture. When the estimated due date approached with no signs of pregnancy, rumor swiftly

219

replaced fact: Ella had 'lost' her half-breed baby, a secret kept by the Howells out of misplaced loyalty. Now the poor girl's path to depravity, a downward spiral, would lead to whoring.

Ella had unwittingly made a mistake when she had related everything that happened to her, speaking freely of her captivity to anyone who expressed an interest. She later discovered her words were reinterpreted, rearranged, and repeated by settlers who believed the savages were brutes that must be eradicated like vermin. Worse, nearly everyone in Denver believed Ella yearned to join armed settlers in a charge to kill bands of Indians. If only I had the chance, I would kill them all by my own hand.

That was a lie, a fabrication that had never come from her lips, or anyone who knew her. Given the circumstances of her captivity and the murder of her father and aftermath, perhaps she should have felt vindictive. In truth, her emotions were tangled, knotted with contradictions. Throughout her ordeal, she had feared for her life. She felt anger toward Many Bears. She well remembered hostility toward her in the tribe.

In retrospect she thought kindly of the old Ute woman, and regretted injuring her when she had pushed her over the edge of the embankment. And in a recurring dream, Ella observed a little boy, bleeding and terrified, hiding behind a clump of flowering rabbitbrush. Shot in the back by a buffalo hunter, the child lived through the night, only to find his loved ones sprawled on the prairie among the rising shadows of dawn, murdered, all of them scalped and slashed.

'Elly Mae, what was it like?'

She peered into Christina's blue eyes. The answer was complex, not readily framed in words, and far too large for Christina to understand. The preacher's daughter was persistent, though, and over a period of weeks, Ella related everything she could remember to her friend.

'What are the Indians like?'

'I was confined in a lodge . . . .'

'Yes, yes, but what was it like?'

'The Cheyennes have their way of life . . . different from ours . . . they have families . . . homes . . . children who play together, parents who laugh with them . . . .'

'Play,' Christina repeated. 'Savages play?'

Ella nodded.

Later, Christina's bright-eyed interest focused on the days and nights Ella had spent with Seth. She wanted to hear more about their escape and what had happened in a place called Shadow Valley.

Ella had only to close her eyes to remember. From that meadow Eagle Feather had led his warriors back to the encampment on the shore of the blue lake. Seth packed his rucksack and took her out of the great valley. In the following days, he led the way through mountain cañons and out of the hot foothills. They walked toward Denver by day, at night sleeping in one another's arms, as though alone in the world.

At first sight of the burgeoning town on the horizon, Seth bid her good bye. Their eyes met and held. Neither spoke. Then he turned away, his easy stride retracing his route to the mountains.

'Oh, Elly Mae, wasn't it exciting?'

'I was afraid I would die.'

'Oh, yes, I know, I know. But you can tell me. Do tell me. What was Seth like?'

She described him, remembering Zebulon Becker had compared Seth to a lone wolf roaming the far mountains. It was not the answer Christina craved to hear.

'Did you . . . did the two of you? . . . oh, you know . . . .'

Ella knew, and wished she had never entered into this interrogation. 'I know what you mean, Chrissy,' she replied softly. 'The answer is no.'

'Oh, I know you wouldn't ever want to,' Christina said, 'but did he ever . . . I mean, did he ever force himself on you?'

'Chrissy . . . ,' Ella said, and turned away.

From the first day of their friendship

to this moment, Christina had confided her secret: pages excised from a volume of romantic poetry were hidden in her Bible. In excitement born of secrecy, she had read and reread them so often that she could recite smoldering verses from memory: "Gold-throated language of love, as secret and as tempting as a passionate kiss." The "flashing eyes and entwined spirits of the lovers told of dark desires," and "lovers shared stolen embraces, eagerly yielding to secret caresses in their quickening journey to a breathless union."

'Breathless union,' Christina whispered, eyes bright as she smiled at her friend. 'Dark desires.' Christina pulled a tattered paper from her pocket and read a poem she had written, until now never shown to anyone:

His voice rides prairie breezes,
softly whispering, whispering
to me.
Free as the breeze, free is he,
whispering his secret to me.

**He roams the land and sails
the sea
whispering his timeless love
for me.**

★ ★ ★

Foul rumors reached Peter and Jane Howell, tendrils of gossip creeping through the town. One common thread ran through this fabric of hate. Forbidden pleasures, folks said, had turned Ella Mae Campbell to whoring. Now she lifted her dress for any man offering a poke of gold dust or a coin. It was true. Everyone knew . . . .

Several men in the First Brethren congregation took Howell aside. They demanded 'that woman' be excluded from church services. Her presence every Sunday was not only an affront to God-fearing folks, but threatened to destroy the fledgling church.

Howell thanked them for their concern. In his booming voice, he stated the one overriding truth they did not want to hear: 'The rumors are false!'

He offered proof to anyone willing to listen. Since her return, Ella Mae had resided with the Howells in a cabin built by the preacher and Jake Osborne. In addition to living in close quarters day and night, Ella was occupied with daily chores. From egg gathering to cream separating, from butter churning to hand watering vegetable plants in the garden, she worked at far too many tasks from dawn to dark to find the time or the energy to engage in the rumored behavior.

In his Sunday message, Howell identified gossip as a sin. Those who heeded it bowed to Satan. Thus, he defended the character of an 'unnamed young woman walking amongst us.' Eleven families left his congregation *en masse*, a cadre of true believers promising to form their own church.

In human nature, Howell thought, resides a mysterious and perverse force. The more he debunked gossip, the more determined some folks were to believe in scandalous behavior. Old rumors were woven into new tales — more lies than ever. He wondered about it, wondered if it was proof of Satan's existence.

Biblical wisdom directed Howell to avoid fueling the flames of evil. He stopped acknowledging rumors, other than to insist the tales swirling around Ella Mae Campbell were false. Ella Mae herself was in tears after learning of the accusations lodged against her. Howell counseled her. Rumor-mongers did not know her, he said, and no one in Denver had the courage to look her in the eye and speak directly to her.

'Falsehood nourishes fools,' he said, 'and gossip is their bitter drink.'

Last autumn Ella had sold her family's wagon and team of oxen and most of their possessions. She gave the money to the Howells in payment for room and board for an unspecified period of time. As much as the Howells were grateful for cash and for Ella Mae's help with daily chores, and as much as they had welcomed her into their family, Peter and Jane had long assumed she would return to her home in Baltimore, or possibly to Washington. But when they learned she had no family members living in Maryland and no close relatives in Washington, D.C., they better understood her dilemma. She did not want to stay here on the frontier, alone, yet she had no other place to go.

During a long career of preaching from the pulpit, Howell had often delivered a familiar message, one that underpinned his faith: God works in ways mysterious to man. He had often illustrated this principle with colorful parables. Now, that very lesson was hammered home to him when the resolution to Ella's dilemma came from an unexpected source.

Levi Case drove a buckboard to Denver every Saturday for supplies. Jared and Jason followed on horseback. They stayed overnight with Aaron Cahill in a back room of the deadfall. Sunday mornings, the boys' habit was to attend worship services while their father sat with Cahill in cool shadows amid pungent odors of the saloon.

Howell was not fooled by appearances. The two sons of Levi Case were hardly bound by piety or fulfilled spiritually when they joined in the singing of hymns or bowed their heads in open-eyed prayer. Howell watched, and saw their gazes roving from one young daughter of a worshipping family to another. Howell knew all too well what it was that young men prayed for. Jared was the most fervent. He was eagle-eyed. With his hair slicked back and his jaw freshly shaved after a Saturday soak, he stared at Christina more often than the other young women.

After Sunday services, Howell heard jingling harness chains outside his cabin. He opened the door as a buckboard wagon pulled up. Levi Case set the brake. Looping the lines around the handle, he stepped down from the bench seat. Jared and Jason reined their mounts to a halt. They sat their horses, hats shoved up on white foreheads, as they leaned back in the saddles and waited for their father to complete his business here.

'Sir, I know we've had our differences,' Case said, removing his wide-brimmed felt hat as he approached the doorway, 'but as one gentleman to another, I believe we can reach a fair understanding.'

'Fair understanding,' Howell repeated. 'About what?'

'Employment for the girl,' he said, halting.

Howell was mystified. 'Girl?'

'Why, yes,' Case replied. 'The girl who works for you. The Campbell girl.'

Howell stepped through the doorway and escorted the rancher away from the cabin. Well beyond the hearing of Ella, Howell resumed their conversation.

'You may have heard talk about her character,' Howell said.

'Yes, of course,' Case replied. 'Everyone has.'

'The rumors are false,' Howell said. 'She is a virtuous young woman.'

'I know,' Case said.

'You do?'

'My boys tell me you have defended

230

the girl ably,' Case said, 'and not without personal cost. Such a sacrifice is to your great credit. As to her purity of spirit and body, I have no reason to disbelieve you.'

Howell studied him. It was difficult to dislike a man of keen perceptions.

'Now, Preacher Howell,' Case chided, 'surely you did not suspect I came here seeking a brood mare to service studs in my employ.'

Howell shook his head vigorously. 'No. No, of course not.'

In truth, though, that very thought had crossed his mind. He had heard the L-Bar-C was home to numerous ranch hands now. How many, he did not know. But where healthy, vigorous men roam . . . .

'She is plain, but she is a woman,' Howell said, dimly aware that he protested too much.

'I can well assure you of her safety,' Case said.

'And I accept your word,' Howell said. He brought a hand to his chin. 'With no surviving parents to guide Ella Mae's decisions in life, I merely wished to inquire about salary and living quarters. Ella Mae is a hard worker.'

Levi Case said: 'I am prepared to offer her one dollar per day, five days a week. I assume she will honor the Sabbath.'

'Yes,' Howell said.

'Weather permitting then,' Case went on, 'my boys will escort her to your home on Saturdays, and make the return trip Sunday afternoons.'

Howell considered the offer. 'I shall speak to her about this.'

'Fair enough,' Case said. He extended his hand as though completing a business transaction. 'Tell the girl I will return in one week for her answer.'

* * *

They had never argued. Not like this. They had suffered through disagreements and a few cross words since they had first met on the bank of the Mississippi River at St. Joe, but never a fiery dispute. Ella was shocked by the

232

explosion from Christina, utterly amazed. She could do nothing more than stare at her sobbing, red-faced friend.

The worst of it was that Ella had misgivings about working for Mr. Case at all, and she might well have declined the offer if she had not been so strongly encouraged to accept it by Peter and Jane Howell. Opportunities for a girl to earn cash money were rare on the frontier, they pointed out, and five dollars a week was handsome. In the end, Ella told the Howells she would accept the employment on a trial basis.

Outside the cabin that evening, Christina pulled her aside, grabbing at her with surprising force while verbally cutting loose in a volcanic fury.

'You can't! You can't take Jared from me! You can't!'

Flabbergasted, Ella repeated: 'Take him from you.'

'You know what I mean! Just because you are plain does not mean you have to be a dumb ox!'

Ella saw tears welling in her eyes.

'Chrissy, I do not know what you mean.'

'Jared . . . Jared kissed me.'

Ella stared at her.

'It's true,' Christina went on. 'After services last Sunday I showed him my poem and told him it was about him. He kissed me. We're in love.'

Ella had seen lingering gazes exchanged between the two of them, but she was shocked by this revelation — and still mystified by her outburst.

'You can't take him away from me!' she said again.

'Chrissy, listen to me. I will work for Mister Case and live on the ranch for a while. That is all. I have no interest in Jared Case.'

'But . . . but you will see him every day,' she said. 'We both know what will happen . . . .'

'Chrissy,' Ella said, 'who is it you mistrust . . . Jared or me?'

The question was unwelcome, and brought another outburst. Ella watched helplessly as Christina spun away and ran back to the cabin in tears.

* * *

Howell looked up. At an early hour the sky was clear, promising another hot day. Lines slack, he gave the team its head. Ella's brass-cornered steamer trunk was lashed to the back of this borrowed carriage. She and Christina sat in the leather-tufted seat behind him, both young women silent since leaving Denver at dawn.

The thin wheels rolled along twin ruts cutting across the shortgrass prairie from Denver to the L-Bar-C Ranch. This ranch road showed more use than Howell would have guessed. Wheel ruts were deep and wide, half filled with dirt that had been churned to powdery dust by freight outfits. Howell noted tracks left by shod horses were numerous, too. Over the last year he had heard tales of large numbers of Virginia horsemen taking employment on the new ranch. Until now he had dismissed extravagant numbers of men and horses. Maybe the camp tales were accurate, after all, with claims of massive construction on the new ranch and the hiring of armed riders to patrol the boundaries of the sprawling range.

Jane had stayed behind in Denver to care for the animals and keep up with chores. She had packed box lunches for her husband, daughter, and Ella, and sent them off with a lemon-iced cake for their host.

Howell glanced back. The faces of the two young women were shaded by sunbonnets, and lap robes warded off fine dust. At their feet were canteens, rain slickers, and nosebags with oats for the horses.

Howell knew his daughter had been crying. He took this as an indication of dread at her separation from Ella Mae, an interruption in their long friendship. He tried in vain to make conversation and lighten her mood. His efforts were met with silence and a lowered gaze.

Howell wished for an alternative, but knew there was no real choice. Ella Mae Campbell needed to make her own way in life, and the opportunity had presented itself in the person of Levi Case. Howell had reminded his daughter that she would see Ella Mae on Saturday afternoons and Sunday mornings. Christina seemed to find no joy in that.

In the afternoon, domed clouds built castles in the sky. Howell pointed to the west. High over distant mountains the bellies of the great clouds darkened. Lightning bolts flashed amid rumbling thunder.

'Coat up,' he said, and put on his hooded slicker.

In minutes a cool wind swept across his face, and the clouds loosed pea-sized hail. The hailstones raised puffs of dust in the road like bullets. The horses tossed their heads, their backs quickly splotched with a light rainfall.

Howell held the lines taut now. He managed to control the team as the storm blew past with swift, dust-swirling winds. Lasting only minutes, a calm wake was left behind, a certain quietude amid fragrant odors of rain-moistened soil, horse sweat, and warm leather.

Howell inhaled these scents that filled the air in the aftermath of the prairie storm, at once relieved he had succeeded in controlling the team. For as far as he could see, hailstones covered the ground, pellets of ice quickly melting. The day was hot again, the land soon to be dry.

Several miles down range, thunder rumbled. Howell saw more bolts of lightning flash from sky to prairie there. Taking off his slicker, he looked back, seeking good cheer from Christina and Ella Mae as he welcomed the warming sun. Neither smiled. Nor did they look at one another.

In the afternoon Howell topped a rise. He pulled back on the lines. Four horsemen were on the prairie a quarter of a mile ahead. They wheeled, coming toward the carriage at full gallop. Howell halted the team.

'Private land, sir,' the lead rider said, reining up.

If his waxed mustache was an attempt to look older, Howell thought, the immature voice gave him away. Still in his teens by Howell's estimate, the rider was a belligerent youngster.

'Turn back!' he commanded.

'We have traveled from Denver,' Howell said, 'to visit Mister Case.'

The other three riders had halted behind him. All of them were young, Howell saw now, dressed alike in gray wool trousers, tall riding boots, dark shirts under duck jackets, and wide-brimmed hats. Their pistols were not drawn, but hands rested near the grips. The first rider spoke again.

'Sir, you are trespassing on private land. Turn back.'

'I will not turn back,' Howell said. 'Either lead us to Mister Case, or get out of the road and let me pass.'

Now the rider drew his handgun, and the others reached for theirs. 'Sir, we are under orders from Mister Case. If you have a message for him, I will deliver it. Now, turn back.'

'Let me pass,' Howell repeated.

'No, sir!'

'Then shoot us,' Howell said, lifting

the lines. 'You brave men will gun down an unarmed preacher and two young women.'

Doubt crossed the youthful face. Spurring his mount closer, he reached out and grabbed for the lines. Howell pulled back, hard, in a tug-of-war. Spooked by the disturbance, the team shied. Both animals tried to rear.

Christina shrieked in sudden terror as she nearly slid off the seat. Howell glimpsed Ella, grabbing her with one hand while grasping an armrest with her other hand. Christina shrieked again. Ella held on as the carriage rocked violently and canted sideways.

Howell won the tug-of-war, and brought the team under control. Aware Ella had just saved Christina from certain injury, or worse, he saw a plume of dust farther down the road. A lone horseman approached at full gallop. He did not recognize the rider until Christina called out.

'Jared!'

12

'Oh, Jared! Thank goodness! Thank goodness you're here!' Ella heard Christina call out as Jared Case slowed the running Morgan horse. He reined up, raising a hand to his hat brim as his mount slid to a halt. Dust boiled up under man and beast. The mounts of the other riders shied and danced away from this display of horsemanship.

Jared's eyes swept past Ella, lingered briefly on Christina, and came to rest as he met the unblinking gaze of Peter Howell. The preacher spoke in a voice thickened by anger.

'Do these hardcases work for your father?'

Jared eyed him. 'Yes, sir.'

'Explain to me why they found it necessary to draw their guns on us,' he said, 'and threaten us with our lives.'

Jared waved a dismissive hand to the four riders. They had holstered their

241

pistols the moment Christina had called him by his first name. Jared said: 'Go on about your business, gentlemen.'

The young rider with the waxed mustache turned his horse and spurred it, leaving at a canter. The others followed. After they rode away, Jared faced Howell and apologized for their rude behavior. Their orders, he said, directed them to patrol L-Bar-C rangeland, armed and aggressive outriders to match the threat posed by horse thieves and raiding savages.

'We are neither,' Howell said, still angered by the confrontation.

'My father's expecting you,' Jared said. He added: 'We all are. I guess some ranch hands weren't listening when they were informed we would receive guests today.'

Jared tilted his head slightly and cast a brief smile at Christina, a gesture that made him look like a younger version of his father. Ella had noticed him during church services. The youth had filled out, becoming a young man in the year since the westward trek when both he and

Jason were hardly more than scrawny kids. Jared possessed some of his father's assertiveness. Gentlemanly polish would come later.

'Follow me.'

Five miles due north, buildings came into sight when the carriage topped a ridge. Ahead, a fringe of grass marked a creek meandering through a shallow draw. The creek fed into a pond, and an expanse of native grasses stretched out from it. With the approach of the carriage, mallards swam away from a cat-tail-choked bank. On higher ground, across the way, Ella saw a ranch house built of logs and raw pine boards, anchored by a stone chimney, and protected by a shake roof.

The largest structure was a horse barn, standing a hundred yards away, steep-roofed to shed winter snows. Pole corrals held saddle horses. A long bunkhouse was nearby, too, alongside a cook house with a black stovepipe. A second bunkhouse was under construction there, a boxy skeleton of raw pine. Outbuildings, pens, and chicken coops were clustered nearby.

Ella gained a panoramic view of the ranch house when Howell turned the carriage where wheel ruts skirted the pond. She gazed at the one-story building with a long verandah across the front. Painted white with a yard free of weeds, it was flanked by a line of cottonwood saplings. Compared to the tumble-down shacks and makeshift cabins of Denver, this was a palace.

The door to the ranch house swung open as the carriage rolled to a halt at the tie rail. Jared swung down. He looped reins around the rail as Levi Case came out of the house, buttoning his jacket to receive guests. His belly was ample, the fit tight.

'Preacher Howell!' he called out. 'Ladies!'

Howell turned. 'Ranch life seems to agree with you, Levi.'

'Thank you, Preacher.'

Ella watched Howell climb out of the carriage. He moved to her side of the high-wheeled vehicle, and took her hand as she stepped down. Jared strode to the other side of the carriage, reached up, and grasped Christina's hand. She smiled, demurely lowering her gaze as she allowed Jared to help her. Ella noted Howell watched them, brow furrowed.

'Come in, come in!' Case said. 'My boys will tend to your team.'

Ella saw Jason come out of the house. He crossed the porch and slowly descended the steps. He was thin compared to his brother, his face as pale as Jared's was ruddy.

'Hello, Jason,' Ella greeted him.

The youth nodded with a quick glance at her. He joined his brother, and led the team and Jared's saddle mount toward the barn. Ella glimpsed Jared's look back, eyeing Christina as she bent down and pulled the covered cake from its place under the carriage seat.

The deep, resonant voice of Levi Case took Ella's attention away from the brothers. She was impressed by this pastoral scene of swimming ducks and grazing horses, of monarch butterflies and redwing blackbirds flying low in close pursuit.

'Come in, come in,' Case said again, his arm moving to the door in a sweeping motion.

Howell mounted the steps and crossed the verandah to the open door. Pulling a dust-caked hat from his head, he stood aside while Case led the way into the ranch house. Ella and Christina stepped through the doorway after him.

Ella passed through an arched entryway into a drawing room, amazed by the furnished elegance before her eyes. Bull trains from the States had brought more than mere building supplies to this outpost of civilization. The walls were papered and decorated with gold-framed paintings of clipper ships and ocean shore scenes. The floor was covered by a thick Persian carpet in a blood red and maroon pattern.

Both Ella and Christina gawked at a room furnished with cushioned settees, upholstered chairs, polished brass lamps, and a small chandelier of cut crystal. Through a sliding door Ella glimpsed a cherry wood dining table and chairs, places set on white linen.

Wine was served in goblets in the drawing room. The beverage was poured by a young man with large, rough hands that were clearly more accustomed to outdoor work. Red wine, misdirected, sloshed onto Ella's sleeve. The young man's face turned wine red as Case threw a hard look at him, and quickly blotted it up with his handkerchief.

'As you see,' Case confided to Ella, 'a feminine touch is needed here.'

'I've been known to spill a drop or two myself,' Ella said.

Levi Case smiled briefly. After discussing his good fortune in surviving his first winter season on the great prairie, he led his guests and two sons into the dining room. Standing at the head of the table, he announced a supper of Smithfield ham, sweet potatoes, peas, and salad greens. He invited Howell to offer a blessing.

'Please be seated,' he said afterward. The meal was served by two young men, both ranch hands as awkward as the first.

Other than more comments about the weather on this prairie and polite inquiries about old friends from the Brethren Wagon Company, the meal was eaten in protracted silence against a background of sterling silver clinking on bone china. After wolfing down the food, the brothers gazed downward in a fit of shyness, and the young women across the table stared into space in deadly boredom.

Promising the dessert from Missus Howell would be served later, Case stood. So did Howell. The two men retired to the drawing room for brandy and cigars.

'You youngsters are on your own,' Case said with a parting smile at them.

Jared eagerly shoved his chair back, and got to his feet. He invited Ella and Christina — addressing them as 'You ladies . . . ' — outdoors for a walking tour of the home ranch. Ella and Christina cast a look at one another. In that moment Ella saw vast pleasure in the other's eyes, as though a dream had come true for her, or was on the verge of it.

'Why, yes,' Christina said. 'That sounds delightful. Doesn't it, Elly Mae?'

'Yes. Delightful.'

They left the table. Passing through the entryway, Ella overheard Howell ask Levi Case how many men were employed on the ranch.

'With no fences to hold these Morgans, Preacher, they turn wild. Stallions fight for mares with the devil's fury. They steal from each other and flee in bands, their hoofs thundering across this land. It's a full-time job for my men to outsmart those outlaw horses, much less figure out how to contain them.'

The note of pride in his horse herd was unmistakable, Ella noticed, along with the fact that he did not answer the question.

Outside, the light of a setting sun shimmered on the surface of the pond. Water splashed as frogs jumped in. On

249

the far bank a jack rabbit leaped straight up. The big rabbit wheeled and bounded away, ears up as it fled in long, leaping strides until out of sight.

'Give one of those critters wings,' Jared said, 'and he'll fly.'

Christina laughed uproariously. 'Fly! Oh, can't you just picture that? A big jack rabbit flying! Can't you just picture that, Elly Mae?'

Ella replied: 'That would be quite a sight.'

'Oh, Jared,' Christina exclaimed, grasping his arm, 'such wild ideas you have! A jack rabbit flying!'

Ella pretended not to notice when the boys exchanged a look, and Jared jerked his head at his brother. Jason meekly asked her to walk with him, and tugged at her sleeve like an insistent little boy. Jared took Christina's arm, murmuring something about the sunset. They turned and hurried away in the opposite direction, angling toward a stack of lumber where the new bunkhouse was under construction.

* ★ *

Despite the liquor and the relaxed atmosphere in the fine house, neither man spoke freely. Howell glanced around the drawing room, idly examining a portrait of a handsome woman in a black dress. Case confirmed she was his late wife, mother of his two sons, dead of cholera back in Virginia.

'Jason takes after her,' Howell observed.

Case nodded. 'He exhibits some of her traits, too. He's a gentle boy, nowhere near as determined to conquer the world as his brother.'

'Or his father?'

'I suppose so.'

Howell was curious about Case's plans for the future, but he sensed something other than this ranch presently occupied the man's mind. His instincts proved to be true. Case's reason for concern emerged after he drained the snifter.

Levi Case began with a thick layer of flattery. He commented again how

251

much he admired Howell for standing up to the citizenry in defense of Ella Mae Campbell's character. He drew on the cigar, looked at the red glowing coal, and slowly exhaled a cloud of smoke.

'You may have heard rumors about me, Preacher.'

'Rumors?' Howell asked.

Case nodded. 'A man in your position . . . much respected as you are . . . .'

'What rumors?'

'Well, Aaron Cahill has heard talk . . . so have other men of his acquaintance . . . .'

Howell pressed him. 'Just what is the subject of these rumors?'

Case eyed him before replying. 'Slaves working on my ranch.'

'Slaves!' Howell repeated.

'It's a lie,' Case said.

'I should hope so.'

'Tales of the damned,' he mused.

Howell studied his silver-bearded face. 'Sir?'

'As the rumor goes,' Case said, 'I hauled Negroes in covered wagons across

252

the plains just as slavers brought them across the ocean in the holds of ships.' Case leaned forward in his chair, jabbing his cigar in front of him as though warding off enemies. 'Tomorrow morning I shall give you a tour of the place. Every nook and cranny. Explore hills and valleys as you wish. You will see for yourself, Preacher. Not one slave on the place, not even in the cook house.'

'A search is unnecessary,' Howell said.

Case managed a slight smile. 'I make demands on men in my employ, and perhaps someone accused me of being a slave-driver. But no slaves are here. Any man on my payroll is free to draw his time and leave the L-Bar-C. That is the truth, Preacher.'

'I have no reason to doubt you,' Howell said.

Case drew on the cigar again. 'You can set folks straight, once and for all. Can't you?'

'I can try.' Howell was taken aback by his aggrieved tone of voice. Levi Case was a man who gave the appearance of supreme self-confidence. But clearly, these accusations worried him.

'I'm not flying the Stars-and-Bars of the Confederacy, either,' Case added. 'That's another rumor you may put to rest.'

Neither man spoke for a long moment. Howell sensed they were nurturing the same thought. He spoke first. 'It stands between us, doesn't it?'

'What does?' Case asked.

'The war,' Howell said.

They gazed at one another in a silence born of tension, each waiting for the other to speak.

'All the way out here in this remote territory,' Howell said at last, 'the war between the states stands between us.'

'That damned war of Mister Lincoln's,' Case added.

'Lincoln's war?' Howell said. He shook his head. 'Jefferson Davis could end it tomorrow.'

'Sir,' Case said, 'I have long believed war would consume us if your Mister Lincoln were elected President. Well, I was right about that, wasn't I?' He drew on the cigar and exhaled. 'If Mister Lincoln has his druthers, we'll all lose our way of life, not to mention our sacred right to own property, too.'

'Human property, you mean,' Howell said.

'Slaves!' Case exclaimed. 'Is that all you Yankees can bellow about?' Exasperated, he added: 'No one dares speak of slaveholders in the North, do they?'

'Slavery does not exist in the North.'

'Sir, you are misinformed.'

'In what possible way?'

'Tens of thousands of half-starved factory and mill workers,' Case replied, 'will gladly tell you about slavery.'

'I do not know what you are suggesting,' Howell said. 'Do you?'

'I am talking about common knowledge,' Case said.

Howell shook his head slowly. 'Tell me about this common knowledge.'

'In the North men are enslaved by low wages,' Case replied, 'that hold entire families on the edge of starvation. Families live in squalor. In the South, workers are well-fed. Families are housed in decent quarters, not city slums bearing sickness and stench . . . .'

'In the North,' Howell countered, 'workers are not sold like cattle, they are not whipped or branded, and they are free to come and go as they wish.'

'Free!' Case scoffed.

'Free to leave,' Howell repeated.

'But how can they?' Case retorted. 'They don't have the means to leave. Your workers have no choice but to labor day and night, enslaved by the wealthy bastards who own those filthy, smoke-belching factories and window-less mills.'

Howell studied him, wishing only to end this argument. More than the war stood between them, he realized now. He did not fully trust him, for in the back of his mind echoed the man's empty prom-ise. After the attack on the wagon train, Levi Case had promised 'on my honor as a gentleman' to aid in the rescue of Ella Mae Campbell from the savages.

Now to employ her and to watch out for her safety — empty promises, too?

★ ★ ★

Ella feigned interest in Jason's boastful ramblings about the benefits of life on the ranch, words he had no doubt heard from his father. Like the great plantations of the South, Jason stated grandly, the L-Bar-C in the West was nearly self-sufficient — fresh water, a food supply, secure housing, workers, livestock.

When Jason ran dry on that topic, he again emulated his father by talking about horses. The stallions were mighty, the mares mighty willing. L-Bar-C Morgans were the best of the breed, he said. The strong, short-coupled horses identified by small, pointed ears and large eyes ran like the prairie wind.

Ella half listened while looking around. She had to agree. A beautiful place, this grass-filled draw was protected from winter snows and summer cyclones, a piece of the American frontier offering prosperity. She thought of her father, of his dreams for a new life out here . . . .

They sat in wicker chairs on the porch, swatting mosquitoes until nightfall. At her request, Jason took her indoors. From the entryway she noticed Mr. Howell and Mr. Case seated in the drawing room, reading newspapers Howell had brought from Denver. She bid them good night.

Jason escorted her to a spare bedroom at the end of a narrow hallway. He and Jared had carried in her trunk before supper. A brass bed, dresser, and wash-stand were here. She would share the bed with Christina tonight, Jason told her, and afterward this room would be her quarters. He turned and left, closing the door.

Ella washed. She changed into night-clothes, and combed out her hair in vigorous strokes. Seeing her image in the mirror triggered a memory; a small half-moon scar under her eye marked the place where the stone thrown by Many Bears had struck her. She was no longer a captive, but the tangled memories would always be with her. Blowing out the lamp, she crawled into bed and stretched her sore muscles.

She was weary from a long day. This soft mattress was luxurious compared to her pallet on the dirt floor of the Howells' cabin. Coming to work here felt like the right decision after all, she thought, remembering a fine supper and cheerful host. She planned to save her wages until she had enough money to strike out on her own — to do what, she did not know. Or where, either. She sensed the future held something for her, that she would be ready for opportunity at the right time. She closed her eyes.

The memory triggered by the mirror image brought more thoughts of the past to her mind. She remembered a place that seemed almost imaginary now — Shadow Valley. The deep gorge was lush with grass and game, a place where fine mist filled the air with rainbows arching over crashing creeks. And Seth was there . . . .

Outside her door, floorboards creaked.

Eyes opening, Ella raised up on an elbow. By starlight seeping through curtains, she saw the bedroom door ease open.

Christina slipped in. She closed the door. Ella heard a muffled sound — a pained sob. She sat up.

'What's wrong? Chrissy, what's wrong?'

Christina gasped, struggling for breath as she made her way through an unfamiliar room in semi-darkness. The bed rocked when she fell across the mattress.

'Chrissy,' Ella whispered again, 'what's wrong?'

She sobbed again. 'I . . . I didn't know . . . it would hurt . . . .'

'Hurt?' Ella asked. 'What hurts?'

'Oh, God, Elly Mae, it hurt.'

'What are you talking about?' Ella could not see her face in this dim light, but when Christina answered with more sobs, suddenly she knew. 'You . . . you and Jared?'

'Yes,' Christina said. 'Oh, Elly Mae, I didn't know it would hurt so much.'

'Are you bleeding?' Ella asked.

'A little,' Christina said.

'I'll get a lamp.'

'No!' Christina said sharply. 'I . . . I don't want to awaken anyone. I'm . . . I'm all right.'

'You're certain?' Ella asked. She moved closer, sitting beside her on the mattress.

'Oh, Elly Mae, I hate myself, I truly hate myself. I just want to take these clothes . . . take them and throw them away . . . or burn them.'

'Did Jared force himself on you?'

'No, no,' Christina said. 'He did not force me to do anything . . . .' She slowly sat up. 'What am I going to do, Elly Mae?' Without waiting for a reply, Christina said urgently: 'No one must know . . . ever. Promise. You have to promise me . . . .'

Ella promised to keep the confidence, but a larger issue loomed before Christina, one that neither of them had to say aloud to acknowledge.

★ ★ ★

In the first pink light of sunrise Peter Howell stood beside the borrowed carriage. He took the outstretched hand of Levi Case, and bid the man farewell.

'I hope you will accept my apology, Preacher.'

Howell eyed him. 'Apology?'

'My father and Grandfather Case,' he explained, 'fine gentlemen that they were, would never have permitted an argument with a house guest. That would be rude and forbidden. The Case men were reserved and polite, always. Well, I was rude toward you last night, Preacher . . . inexcusably rude. I sincerely apologize for my behavior.'

'Apology accepted,' Howell said. 'But we both know your father and grandfather, in their eras, did not live through a war raging between the states like a wildfire. Passions run deep nowadays, and it is most difficult to hold one's temper.'

'Well stated, Preacher.' He paused. 'About that matter we discussed last evening . . . .'

'Matter?'

'Well, you've seen the place,' he reminded him, and lowered his voice. 'No slaves are here.'

'I know that to be true, Levi.'

'Thank you.'

The door to the ranch house opened. Howell turned. He saw his daughter come out. She crossed the porch, arm in arm, with Ella. They descended the steps together. Howell glimpsed his daughter's eyes. They were reddened by tears.

'Close friends,' he confided to Case as the pair walked slowly toward them. 'This separation is hard on them, particularly Christina.'

'Well, I shall hold up my end of the bargain, as we agreed,' Case said. 'Either I or one of my boys will drive Miss Campbell to your home Saturdays, and bring her back here on Sundays as we agreed.'

Case glanced around, frowning. 'Speaking of rude behavior, where are those boys of mine? They readied your team, and disappeared. They should be out here bidding good bye to our guests.' He turned to Howell and added helplessly: 'They will remember this while mucking out barn stalls all day in the company of horseflies and mosquitoes, you may be certain of that.'

Howell chuckled. 'Don't be too hard on them, Levi. They're good boys.'

'Most of the time,' Case allowed. 'Most of the time.'

Howell handed Christina up to the seat, walked around the vehicle, and climbed in. Taking up the lines, he turned the carriage and drove out of the yard, rounding the pond. Looking back, he saw Case lift a hand in parting. Ella stood at the man's side, her gaze fixed on Christina in the departing carriage.

13

Ella had been cautioned by Peter Howell, and she discovered he was right. Levi Case was a harsh taskmaster. He was neither mean nor cruel. But if the adage was true — two kinds of men trod the earth, the drivers and the driven — then Levi Case was a driver.

Her job was not to prepare food, but to serve it according to Case's whim. He required the table to be set with polished silver, clean crystal stemware, and pressed napkins neatly folded into fourths with the monogram showing. Soup and then steaming hot food were to be served promptly after he took his place at the head of his table. If supper was not ready, the cooks down at the ranch's cook house soon heard about it. Like the king of the realm, Levi Case was all powerful on the L-Bar-C. He ruled his sons, and Ella supposed he ruled ranch hands with the same zeal. She did not venture to the bunkhouse to find out.

Case had lectured her about wandering. For the most part she was not to leave the house. Her private spaces outdoors were limited to the verandah and the toilet, with an occasional stroll to the pond if the riders were gone for the day.

'The men who ride for this ranch are honorable Virginians, Miss Campbell,' Case said to her, 'and they are required to live by a code of conduct. Those who violate it are sent packing. But you are a woman, and they are men, and we all know what can happen if we are not vigilant. I understand this is confining for you, and, if you find the arrangement to be unacceptable, you may terminate your employment. I do not mean that to be a threat, Miss Campbell. It is a simple fact. I will not allow my riders to fraternize with you, nor you with them.'

She also learned Levi Case was mellowed by alcohol. Evenings found him to be in good humor; mornings he growled. Ella recalled a joke told by friends of her mother a long time ago: 'You never truly know a man until you have seen him when he first awakens in the morning, and by then you are shackled by a wedding band and, good-humored or ill-tempered, you are stuck with him.'

In a screened room at the back of the house Ella washed clothing and bedding. She ironed and folded and prayed for a breeze. In the house she dusted, cleaned furnishings, swept, filled lamps. If any of her tasks were not performed to Case's liking, he was quick to criticize. She understood why his sons were quiet, avoiding eye contact with their father as though a bold look cast in his direction from either of them would trigger a new set of orders — or wrath.

Jared and Jason treated her with courtesy. They were circumspect, usually. She caught Jared staring at her a few times, not aggressively, but clearly trying to divine something. She figured he was wondering if Christina had confided in her, and he wanted to read her thoughts to find out how much she knew.

During that first month of her

employment she was taken to Denver every Saturday. In a routine that became familiar, Jared and Jason dropped off their father at Cahill's saloon, and drove the buckboard on to the Howell cabin. Leaving Ella there, they went to Rocky Mountain & Co., a supply store, and filled out the J-Bar-C list. On Sunday they returned to the ranch. Neither Jared nor Jason attended Howell's church services any longer.

Walking arm in arm by the muddy bank of the river, Ella spoke privately to Christina. She failed to cheer her. Christina's mood sank from morose to a sullen melancholy when she confided her fear that she was pregnant.

'I have betrayed my parents and everything we believe in,' she whispered, head bowed. 'All I could think about was losing Jared . . . losing him to you . . . .'

Christina did not ask about him, and Ella offered no details about her life on the ranch. The worst moment for her came when Jane took her aside. Tears welling in a mother's eyes, she asked what was wrong with her daughter.

Ella remembered her promise to Christina. She kept it. She claimed not to know, even though telling a lie as a matter of honor was troubling to her. She felt she had to lie. Besides, if Christina's worst fear came true, her mother would know in due time.

Over supper Ella answered routine questions from Peter Howell. Yes, she was treated well on the ranch. Yes, she was paid as promised. Yes, she was well-fed. Yes, the ranch was a busy enterprise.

At first, Howell doubted the numbers of men she reported riding for the L-Bar-C. Ella insisted she had counted correctly — twenty-five. In addition, the second bunkhouse had been completed. From snatches of overhead conversations, she learned more riders were expected from Virginia.

Howell slowly shook his head as he thought about that. 'I'm not a rancher, but I know that many riders are not needed to run a horse and cattle operation, even a big, unfenced spread. And if the other bunkhouse is filled, the number of L-Bar-C riders will double. Am I right about that, Ella Mae?'

She nodded.

Howell turned from her and stared off into space.

* ★ ★

One hot month stretched into two. The dog days of summer yielded to the winds of autumn. Breezes swept out of the north, slowly cooling the Great Plains.

As Ella had hoped, when she had accepted this job, she was able to save nearly all of her wages. She worked long hours, and it was drudgery, a never-ending cycle of washing, mending, mopping. She polished everything from candlesticks to silverware, black boots to brass buckles. Even though she was lonely and missed feminine company, the money she earned kept her spirits up. Someday she would have enough to leave this place and make a life for herself.

In spare moments Ella cut and sewed

fabric purchased in Denver. She made aprons, a new dress, and a divided riding skirt, the latter with a hope she would be allowed to ride horseback on the ranch someday. While threading a needle or carefully cutting fabric on the bias, she sometimes found herself wishing her mother were here to help her. Routine tasks often brought thoughts of her parents to mind. Quietly shedding tears in those moments, she wondered what her life would be like if her mother and father had survived the trek west.

Ella had learned to listen for approaching horses at sunset. L-Bar-C riders usually returned to the home ranch between sundown and nightfall. The rumble of hoofbeats set in motion a series of events as the men came in. While Case and his sons tended their mounts down at the corrals, their meals were carried up from the cook house. The shrill squeal of the pump handle outside was Ella's signal to fill water glasses, uncover the soup tureen, and set out crackers with freshly churned butter. Soon the three of them would troop into the house. Hatless and still wet from washing up at the pump, the father and sons took their places at the fine table, silent, tired, famished.

Ella became aware of increased numbers of riders coming and going. They were all dressed in similar clothing, the garb of Westerners — wool trousers, flannel shirts, vests, jackets of cotton duck, riding boots, and stockmen's hats. Armed with handguns in holsters and muskets in saddle scabbards, they departed the home ranch in groups. When a pair of horse-drawn supply wagons accompanied them, Ella knew the men would not return to the home ranch for several days, or even a week.

She was never told when Levi Case and the riders would come back, where they had gone, or what they did. Her tasks centered around cleaning the house and having meals ready at a moment's notice. It was woman's work, and she was to be quiet and quick about it. Man's work was for men, Levi Case stated, and politics a man's domain, not a proper subject for women to discuss or attempt to understand. Early on, one severe look from him informed her such conversations were not for her ears, that questions or comments were not to pass through her lips.

His heavy-handed rule pained her. Since her youth, Ella and her father had had many such discussions. She had been taught to trust her powers of reason, and at home she had been expected to think about the larger issues of life.

With all the talk of war at the dinner table, Ella remembered her father's strong opinions. If war between the states erupted, he had believed fighting would sweep through Maryland. The Rebels would attempt to sack Washington just as British redcoats had burned the capital half a century ago. Earl Campbell had believed wars solved nothing, that bloodied adversaries wound up negotiating peace treaties after the smoke had settled — after young men had sacrificed their lives to advance the negotiating positions of politicians.

It had been another reason for the family to leave Maryland. Her father had believed a civil war, if one came, would not spread out to the territories where the population was sparse and secession not an issue.

Ella had overheard Jason gripe about endless 'drills,' but she did not know what the term meant. The younger son complained frequently. Jared never complained. He eagerly rode with the men, often in the lead with his father, sometimes leaving his brother behind, 'feeling poorly,' to spend the day in his room. From her bedroom window, one morning, Ella counted fifty-two men on horseback.

On occasion a visitor from town rode to the ranch, a fair, diminutive man coming in fast on a blaze-faced Morgan gelding. Welcomed by Levi Case, the pair was soon engaged in hushed conversation. This man usually stayed for supper and spent the night. He was balding and fine-featured with a thin mustache and trimmed sideburns. His voice was soft, almost feminine, his gestures cat-like.

Ella did not know him, and she was not introduced to him as she served their meals. She overheard Levi Case variously address him as 'Mister Cahill,' and 'Colonel Cahill.' She recalled hearing that surname. It had been mentioned by Howell and others from time to time. Aaron Cahill owned a deadfall in Denver, the saloon Jake Osborne referred to as 'a nest of Rebs.'

When she left the dining room, Ella had noticed, the subject of their discussions turned from horses and weather to the war raging between the states. There had been setbacks, Cahill allowed, but in the major battles, Southerners were victorious. The Yankees would be turned back, sent fleeing for safety behind the skirts of their mothers and wives.

One day late in the second month of her employment on the ranch, she saw Cahill arrive from Denver at a gallop, and this time, when he reached the ranch, the level of excitement was suddenly elevated. Jared ran to the bunkhouses. Moments later cheers erupted. Ella overheard bits and pieces, without making much sense of them.

'We've got orders, gentlemen!'

'The hour is at hand!'

'A second front for the cause!'

Levi Case took her aside after supper. His face was flushed, his breath reeking of whisky. He made a strange request, strange and deferential as though humbly requesting a personal favor.

'Miss Campbell, would you mind retiring to your room and remaining there for the rest of the night? We shall take breakfast as usual with an extra place set for our guest.'

Ella nodded without comment. She did not know why the request had been made, but she knew better than to ask. She had overhead enough to know that man, Cahill, had made a hard ride from Denver for the express purpose of addressing the men tonight. They were 'under orders' to gather in the barn.

She was not prepared, though, for what she saw when she pulled her bedroom curtain aside at dusk. Crossing the yard on their way to the great barn, Levi Case and his sons strode step for step with Aaron Cahill. Now the saloon man wore a military officer's uniform — gray with black trim. Armed with a saber on his belt, opposite a holstered revolver, he sported a gray felt campaign hat with a plume. He carried a flagstaff. Upon reaching the barn, Cahill unfurled the Stars and Bars of the Confederacy.

An armed man waited at the double doors of the horse barn. Ella recognized him even from this distance. He was the young man with the waxed mustache who had confronted them the first time Peter Howell had traveled the road to the L-Bar-C Ranch.

Now the young man snapped to attention, presenting his musket. With the salute returned, he turned and pulled open one of the doors leading into the cavernous barn. High-pitched yells erupted when the four of them entered. Cahill thrust the flag aloft. A second, louder, chorus of Rebel yells came from the men in the barn, their voices drifting to Ella's window.

After breakfast, the next morning, Cahill set out from the ranch, this time leading a saddle mount bearing the L-Bar-C brand. He returned the next day, followed by a shaggy, poorly dressed man riding that spare horse.

Ella heard the guest tromp into the house where he was welcomed by Levi Case. A shiver ran up her back the moment a rough voice bearing curses boomed down the hall. She had not heard that voice since she had been confined to a teepee in the Cheyenne encampment on the shore of the blue lake. It was Zebulon Becker.

* * *

'He lied to me. Mister Levi Case looked me straight in the eye, and lied.'

Howell's hushed response to Ella's account of events on the ranch during the previous week gave full measure of the betrayal he felt. The more he thought

278

about it, the more he realized the pieces fit together to make a complete picture.

'Levi Case implored me to speak from the pulpit,' he said, 'to assure folks no slaves were on his land. I see his purpose now. Slaveholding was not the issue. He meant to discourage Northern sympathizers from riding out there to see for themselves . . . and catch sight of a regiment of Virginia volunteers.'

That much was clear to Howell. Aaron Cahill called himself 'Colonel,' packed a Confederate uniform in his bag, and used Case's L-Bar-C as a staging area. Large numbers of armed men were training out there, no doubt practicing field exercises on the far reaches of the prairie, all of them unseen by outsiders.

Howell deduced that much from Ella's account. But why? The purpose behind training a regiment of Southerners on the Western frontier was a mystery. And one piece of the puzzle certainly did not fit: Zebulon Becker. Why bring Becker to the ranch? If Levi Case was half the judge of men as he was of horseflesh,

Howell could not imagine one reason for him having anything to do with a reprobate loyal to the highest bidder.

Ella provided the answer to his question. She described Becker's arrival. As usual, Case had not introduced her to the guest, and Becker did not recognize her when she served their supper. She looked quite different from the last time the trader had seen her — buckskin dress, hair matted, bruised and dirty from head to toe. Now she wore a long dress under an apron decorated with fine lace, and her hair was pulled up into a bun under a white cloth maid's cap. She was aware of Becker's leering stares that evening, at once relieved to see no recognition in his eyes.

With Case and Cahill looking on in equal parts of disgust and fascination, Becker ate with his fingers. He tore cooked beefsteak apart as he pinned the meat down to the china plate with the point of his knife clenched in his free hand. Finished, he wiped the blade clean on the folded napkin beside his plate and sheathed it. As an afterthought, he rubbed his greasy hands on his trouser legs. Muttering a complaint of sore teeth, he lifted his gaze and blinked, just then aware of silence at the dinner table.

'Good chow,' he said. He belched over the empty plate and smacked his lips like a hound. 'God-damned good chow.'

Becker left the ranch house, stumbling drunk, after downing five snifters of brandy. He had been told to bunk with the riders. His foul odor, though, got him a quick eviction from the bunkhouse, with the men threatening to heave him into the pond. Met with an explosion of curses and promises of violence, the L-Bar-C riders settled for escorting the trader into the barn. They shoved him, stumbling, into the runway and closed the big doors as though that would hold him.

Ella was able to answer Howell's question because she had edged out of her room and slipped down the hallway in bare feet. She had overheard Levi Case and Aaron Cahill on the verandah. The pair smoked cigars, chuckling, while

Zebulon Becker was pushed from the bunkhouse toward the pond, and then reversed course to the barn, loudly cursing all the way.

'A cruder man I have never encountered,' Case said.

'He eats like a starved weasel,' Cahill said, 'and speaks like some escapee from an asylum.'

'Can we trust him?' Case asked.

'Hell, no,' Cahill replied. He paused. 'But I suppose we must. For now.'

'Well, he seems to know the savages,' Case said.

Cahill said: 'He says the going rate for a muzzleloader is five buffalo robes, but some tribesmen won't carry a gun. Seems they have taboos against touching steel.'

Case said: 'Well, he claims he can bring us an interpreter.'

'One that is fluent in the language of the Cheyenne tribes,' Cahill insisted. 'Not mere hand signals. I made that clear to him. We need a man who speaks the words of their language.'

'Well,' Case said, 'Becker won't receive that hundred-dollar fee until he delivers.'

'Not one damned penny,' Cahill agreed. 'Cash is the only leverage a man like that respects.'

★ ★ ★

Ella thought of the damp bed sheets pinned to the clothesline as clouds began blocking out the sunlight. Aware of sudden shadows early in the afternoon, she dashed outside. She grabbed six white sheets off the line behind the ranch house moments before a dust-laden wind blew into the draw.

Sprinting inside, she threw the sheets across the dining room table, and hurriedly closed the windows. As usual, the storm came and went in a matter of minutes. She had dusted and swept this morning, and now she walked through the house with a sense of dread. Hard-earned experience had taught her that hours of work could be undone in minutes by a prairie storm.

Dust dulled freshly mopped floors. Just enough dust, she thought, to catch Mr. Case's critical eye. She drew a deep breath. She would have to mop again. But at least the sheets were clean, and she would not have to wash them a second time.

When the sun reappeared, Ella took the sheets outside and hung them on the line again. In the house she stoked a fire and heated flatirons. The cotton sheets would soon dry, and then she could start her ironing. In this climate everything dried quickly, she had discovered, everything from wet laundry to fresh bread. Her skin flaked dry, too, and after a wash her hair looked like it had exploded. When combing her unruly hair before a mirror, she sometimes recalled memories of the Ute woman kneading bear grease into it.

Now Ella stepped into the front hallway, mop in hand. After the confusion of those windswept moments, she discovered she had left the door to her room standing open. Or had she? Her gaze went to the floor, untouched since the brief storm. Now she saw boot prints in a coating of dust. A chill ran up her back.

Ella paused. She heard no sounds. She did not sense the presence of another person in this house. Jason was not here. He had left with the riders early this morning. She was alone. But those boot prints were clear evidence. Even though she could not quite believe it, someone had been here in the last few minutes.

Moving slowly toward her door, she paused, heart pounding. She edged closer, paused again, and stepped into the doorway. She leaned in and looked in every corner. Then she entered and knelt as she probed under the bed with the mop handle. The room was empty.

She stood. Her eyes went to the window. It was open.

Fear surged through her. Moments ago, whoever had been here had left by that window. Her first instinct was to close it. She crossed the room and shut it, hard. She turned, her back to the wall. Her gaze went to the top of the dresser by her bed. A rounded, gold object was there.

Ella crossed the room to the dresser in long strides. Picking up the gold pocket watch, she immediately recognized the timepiece carried by her father. Pressing the release confirmed it — **Beloved Husband . . . Devoted Wife**.

Suddenly light-headed, she slumped down on the bed, staring at her father's pocket watch. Who had brought it here? The last time she saw it, the timepiece had been in the possession of Eagle Feather. Had Zebulon Becker traded for it?

When she thought about the boot tracks in the dust, she recalled the conversation she had overheard between Mr. Case and Mr. Cahill. They had sent Becker for an interpreter.

Seth. Had he been here, she wondered, entering as silently as a cloud shadow in those moments of the windstorm?

14

Ella spent more time on the verandah than usual. While she was not entirely guilty of the flirtation Mister Case had warned her to avoid, in truth, she wanted to catch a certain man's eye.

The more she thought about it, the more she came to believe it was Seth who had left the pocket watch in her room. For one thing, Zebulon Becker was simply incapable of moving swiftly or quietly. For another, he was not a man to give away anything of value, certainly not a gold timepiece.

Ella left her sewing basket by the wicker chair on the verandah to feed dried breadcrumbs to the ducks in the pond. If Seth was close by, watching, she hoped he would see she was alone and approach the house. She did not know why he had slipped away, other than the fact that he was more than half wild and probably felt trapped when he stepped into any house. As she thought more about it, she realized Seth could have been here last night, too, observing the ranch house from outdoors as lamps had been extinguished by four people turning in for the night. How else could he have known which room was hers?

By sundown she was convinced he was not in the area, and went into the house. She was setting the table in the dining room when she heard the rumble of a heavy wagon rolling into the draw on the rutted ranch road. She went to the window and peered out. Not a rancher's buckboard, but a big freight wagon pulled by four draft horses was rolling by the pond. The whip-wielding teamster headed for the horse barn, followed by Aaron Cahill on horseback. Ella noticed the wagon box was tightly covered with new canvas.

Within an hour L-Bar-C riders came in from the opposite direction. They were led by Levi Case, with his sons close behind. Ella saw Case rein up and dismount, handing the reins to Jason.

Levi Case met Cahill near the barn door where the teamster had halted the freight outfit. While Jared and Jason moved to the corral with the horses, Cahill loosened a line securing the canvas cover. He pulled it back to reveal the contents of the wagon box to Case.

From her place in the ranch house, Ella could not see what made the rancher nod approval. She watched Cahill close the canvas, drawing it tightly and tying the line. Then she spotted a shaggy figure edging around the corner of the barn. Even from this distance she heard rough cursing, and knew Zebulon Becker had returned.

After a brief conversation with Case and Cahill at the barn, Becker turned and walked away. Clearly he was not invited to dinner this evening, for Mr. Case and his sons headed to the house with Cahill. Ella stepped back from the window.

Saturday she traveled to Denver as usual. This time both Jared and Jason drove empty supply wagons from the ranch — two hard-bouncing buckboards rattling the occupants' teeth all the way across the prairie to Denver. Their father and Cahill accompanied them on horseback.

Ella rode with Jason. In town, Levi Case and Aaron Cahill went to the saloon. Jared swung away and headed for the general store, giving the Howell cabin a wide berth. He need not have.

After greeting Peter and Jane Howell, Ella shook the dust from her bonnet and went for a walk with Christina. They made their way, arm in arm, through tall grass to a sandbar on the riverbank. Christina abruptly stopped and faced her. For the first time in a long while Ella saw a smile on her friend's face. She guessed the news before Christina said it aloud.

'Elly Mae, I'm not pregnant.'

Life was good again, and Christina walked with a light step. She said she had hated lying to her parents in answer to their gentle questions about the dark mood that had settled over her like an evil spell, but she felt worse about the prospect of telling them the truth. She knew they would be hurt as never before. As it turned out, Peter and Jane would never find out about their daughter's tryst with Jared Case, and the whole mess, as Christina said now with a quick laugh, was best left behind to draw flies like a fresh cow patty in a wet pasture.

Over supper, Ella answered Peter Howell's questions about life on the L-Bar-C. He was particularly interested in the arrival of the freight wagon and its cargo. When Ella could not even hazard a guess as to the contents of the wagon box, Howell leaned closer to her.

'Can you find out?'

His question shocked her, the ramifications immediately apparent. Howell was not asking her to question Mr. Case. He was asking her to spy on him.

Howell saw Ella Mae's eyebrows lift. He could see she was surprised. More than surprised — amazed. He had never made such a request of her before, and now they eyed one another for a long moment. He did not want her to risk life and limb, but, on the other hand, the stakes were high and the time to act was drawing near.

Ella said slowly: 'My place is in the ranch house. I have never been down to the barn before . . . or even close to it.'

'I understand,' Howell said. 'Mister Case isolates you from the men for your own well-being. Am I right about that?'

'Yes,' Ella replied.

'I would never ask you to compromise your safety,' Howell said. He thought about that. 'Would it be possible for you to get close to that freight outfit during the day while Case and the riders are gone?'

Ella nodded slowly. 'I guess I could. I'd have to watch out for the cooks and the helpers.'

'But you can slip past them?' Howell asked.

Ella nodded again, knowing that was easier said than done. Every day four men were singled out for duty as the cooks' helpers. They labored at tasks ranging from woodcutting to potato peeling to pot washing. Much of their time was spent with chores in the cook house, but she had no way of knowing when one or more would step outside to roll a smoke or fill a pipe bowl and kneel in the shade outside.

'This is of utmost importance,' Howell said.

Ella heard a grave tone in his voice.

He went on: 'You know Levi Case lied to me, don't you?'

Ella nodded.

'Now I know his reason,' he said.

'What is it?' she asked.

'In war,' Howell answered, 'any lie is justified so long as it brings victory closer.'

'War?' Ella said.

'From all evidence, it seems clear enough Case and Cahill have declared war.'

'What do you mean?'

'You witnessed an act of treason when you saw the Stars and Bars unfurled by a man wearing a Confederate uniform,'

293

Howell replied. 'You've seen fifty armed men on the ranch. You've overheard young Jason complain about 'drills'.'

She met his gaze.

'Ella Mae,' Howell said, 'I don't know what their plan is, but we have every reason to believe some sort of military action is imminent.'

'What kind of action?'

'Perhaps they mean to attack Denver and capture it for the South,' Howell said. 'Or perhaps they have in mind some sort of hit-and-run attack . . . or a series of attacks. Acts of violence in the Western territories will pull troops away from battlefields back East. Perhaps that is their goal.'

While Ella listened, she thought of her father's belief that a civil war would not spread to the far frontier. She also remembered he had often stated his belief that war fever was a terrible disease poisoning the minds of good men. Now Ella wondered if that fever was infecting 'good men' out here in Colorado Territory. Certainly it had already pitted Howell against Case.

'I don't know what Levi Case and Aaron Cahill are planning,' Howell repeated, 'but I know enough to notify the territorial governor of a Rebel force operating freely within Federal boundaries. As you may remember, Ella Mae, troops were requested for law enforcement purposes some time ago. I have no doubt the urgency of this latest information will bring bluecoats on the run.'

★ ★ ★

Ella's hand shook. She aimed the long spout of the silver pitcher, but missed the cup and sloshed coffee into the saucer and onto the tablecloth in front of Mr. Case's plate. He cast a severe look at her, but said nothing. She quickly apologized for her clumsiness and blotted up the spill with a napkin.

She was surprised by her own nervousness this morning. Breakfast chores were the same as before, a well-practiced routine, yet, overnight, everything had changed. Now she was hiding a secret. She had not slept well. Howell's words kept running through her mind. If what he said proved to be true, how much longer could she stay on the L-Bar-C?

Ella could not stop thinking about the war raging between the states. Before yesterday news of battles and casualty figures had been vague and distant, unreal. Now the war was all too real, as close as this stern, stout man occupying the head of his table.

L-Bar-C riders saddled up and left the corrals that morning, led as usual by Levi Case and his sons. When drumming hoof beats died out, she heard the sounds of an axe blade cutting into wood. From a window in the house, Ella saw one of the men chopping firewood for the day. The other three were inside the cook house, preparing supper for this evening and packing box lunches for the next day. Ella worked at her usual cleaning tasks, but on this day she kept an eye out the south-facing windows.

She saw that the freight outfit had been

moved to the side of the barn last night. To her good fortune, it was out of the line of vision of anyone in the cook house now. If she could somehow walk there without being seen, she could examine the cargo and return to the house in a matter of a few minutes.

Somehow. Wild notions charged through her mind. She thought of starting a grass fire to distract the men in the cook house, but quickly gave that up as she remembered the wind storm and imagined the whole ranch going up in flames. She considered running to the cook house to report a glimpse of savages beyond the rise. If the men grabbed up their guns and ran in the direction she pointed, and if they were gone long enough for her to rush down to the freight outfit . . . .

Too many ifs. In the end, she decided simply to step outside and descend the steps of the verandah, walk past the pond, and stroll to the barn. She would act as if she was free to come and go like anyone else. After all, it was unlikely the riders knew she was not supposed to leave the house. All they knew was that the ranch house and immediate area were off limits to them. If she acted like she knew what she was doing, she could walk purposefully to the barn and return without raising suspicion. So she hoped.

She put on her bonnet, cast a look at herself in the mirror where she saw a guilty face, and headed down the hall to the front door. She had decided to get this task over with today. Who knew what tomorrow would bring? The freight wagon might be moved again, or the teamster might even drive it away. Or tomorrow Jason might decide to stay at the ranch.

With a last tug at the silk strap of her bonnet, she left the house. Midday was bright and sunny and hot. She made her way around the edge of the pond. Ducks quacked at her. Redwing blackbirds swept out of a stand of cat-tails, showing scarlet patches on their wings as they darted overhead in their flight.

Ella paused. She cast a glance toward

the cook house. In the heat of the day none of the men was outdoors.

Ducks paddled vigorously toward her, quacking impatiently as though ordering her to drop bread into the water without further delay. After one more glance around her surroundings, Ella turned her back on the raucous ducks. She headed for the barn, heart pounding.

Passing the cook house, she heard men talking inside. As far as she could determine, they were unaware of her. She walked on, angling past the closed doors of the barn. She moved around the corner of the big structure, and strode toward the freight wagon.

Alone and out of sight from the cook house and the two bunkhouses, she hurried to the tailgate. She pulled the canvas up, or tried to. It was tied down snugly. Fingers shaking, she loosened a knot in the line, and managed to raise the canvas a few inches. Sunlight reflected off metal underneath. She pulled more of the canvas free, and peered in. She saw a row of eight or ten muskets in the wagon box, new guns with powder, lead, and bullet molds still in boxes.

'Whut the goddamn hell ye doin', girlie?'

Ella spun around. She came face to face with Zebulon Becker.

The shaggy trader gazed at her, hands on his hips. 'I done axed ye. What're ye doin' here?'

'Mister Case sent me,' was all she could think to say. She smelled him now, and a familiar wave of nausea coursed through her.

'Sent ye to do whut?' Without waiting for her answer, Becker cocked his head. 'Ain't we done met up somewheres? I'm a-thinking we done met up . . . .'

Ella ducked her head as his voice trailed off.

'I'll be good goddamned! Now I recollect! Yer that girlie I seen in the camp by the blue lake, that camp of stinking savages. Ain't ye?'

Ella considered denying it, but quickly saw the futility of lying to him. Becker had that look of triumph in his eye, and no denial from her would take it away.

'Ye lied. Yer pa, he warn't gonna pay me nothing fer bringing ye out, not five hunnert now, not five hunnert later. He's dead, folks says.'

'I didn't know that when I told you . . . .'

He cut her off with a curse. 'So ye ran off with the 'breed. Whut did he do to ye?'

Ella did not reply.

Becker squinted. 'Ye know whut I'm a-talking about.'

'Leave me alone.'

'Ye musta done him, then. Huh? Ye done him proper.'

'I have nothing to say to you.'

'Ye better say plenty, girlie. I done axed ye. Whut ye snoopin' around this here wagon fer?'

'Mister Case sent me,' she said again as she turned to the tailgate and tightened the canvas. She added: 'To make sure this cover will shed rain.'

'One more god-damn' lie,' Becker scoffed. 'Reckon I'll take this to Mister

Levi Case hisself.' He paused. 'Or do ye want me to keep yer secret?'

Ella did not reply.

'How about we keep this here thing between us,' Becker said. 'Huh?'

Ella eyed him, seeing dark holes in his open-mouthed grin.

'Hike up yer skirt fer me, girlie, and ye can do me like ye done that 'breed.'

Ella turned and started to walk away. Becker's hand shot out. He grabbed her arm and pulled her back, hard.

'I dunno whut yer up to,' he said angrily, 'but I got a feeling yer in hot water. If ye want no harm, pull yer god-damn' dress up and drop yer underpants down . . . .'

Wincing against his odor, Ella tried to pull away. His grip tightened. If she screamed, men would come running. But all she wanted was to get away. She struggled mightily as Becker yanked her closer to him. Raising her arm, bent at the elbow, she swung back at him. The point of her elbow caught him squarely in the jaw.

Becker let out a pained whimper, a cry that was almost child-like. Ella thought he would lunge at her. But he slowly sank to his knees, one dirty hand pressed to his jaw, eyes squeezed shut.

'Oh, God, ye done hurt me . . . my teeth, they hurts fierce . . . .'

Ella left him there. She straightened her clothing and hurried back toward the ranch house. In a sidelong glance she saw four men standing outside the cook house, hatless and sweating as they stared at her. They must have heard Becker's voice, and stepped outdoors to see what was causing the commotion. Three white-shirted cooks edged into the doorway behind them.

Head bowed, Ella strode swiftly to the ranch house. In her room she sat down, feeling sick. Levi Case would hear about this. She had no doubt of it.

★ ★ ★

'My brethren, no man may possess another man! Human beings are not to

303

be owned or bartered, any more than they are to be chained or whipped! Human beings are not cattle or pigs or sheep to be bought and sold on a common auction block! My brethren, slavery is more than the greatest injustice of our time! Slavery is a sin. Slavery is a mortal sin. Slavery is a mortal sin against God Almighty! Slaveholders, my brethren, will burn in hell! Slaveholders will burn in hell for eternity!'

Peter Howell raised his Bible in both hands as he delivered this climactic message from the hilltop that Sunday morning. His black coat was wet with sweat, his brow shining. With his wife and daughter looking on, Howell heard shouts from the congregation gathered before him. The power of their voices washed against him like a hot tide.

When he announced his acceptance of God's call to join in the holy crusade, he was met with loud cheers. Inspired, he spoke of the inevitable triumph of right over wrong, of good over evil by soldiers of God Almighty. The cheers swept over him again.

Howell had never felt such exhilaration. The congregation radiated enormous power, as though by some human alchemy the men and women were no longer separate beings, but had joined into one, like molten steel in a forge, steel now coiled in a spring that was flexed and ready to launch them into battle.

Howell lowered his Bible. He looked around. Familiar faces peered at him, among them Jake Osborne and a handful of other men from the original Brethren Wagon Company. Missing from the congregation this morning was Ella Mae. From the L-Bar-C, the young rider with a waxed mustache had delivered a message yesterday.

'Miss Campbell is ill, sir,' he said. 'Nothing serious, but she did not feel up to the journey. She sends word that she will attend services next Sunday, as usual.'

Howell did not believe a word of it. As he watched the cloud of dust billowing behind the rider returning to the ranch, Howell sensed something had happened to Ella Mae.

He had to act. Bluecoat troopers were not here yet, if they were coming at all. There was only one way to ensure her safety, and after his fiery speeches twenty-two armed men with horses were prepared to depart at midnight. Their destination was the L-Bar-C Ranch.

Odd, Howell thought, that he had been unable to raise a militia to rescue Ella Mae Campbell from a tribe of savages, but when the men of his church learned a force of Confederates were training on lands claimed by Levi Case — and Case was rumored to be a slaveholder — they were eager to take up arms and ride into battle, outnumbered or not.

★ ★ ★

'Tell me, Miss Campbell, how long have you been a Yankee spy?'

The question was posed by Levi Case, with his sons and Aaron Cahill looking on. Ella did not answer. She had believed she would be sent away from the ranch, expelled from this place and driven back to Denver with her possessions tossed into her trunk. She was wrong.

'Preacher Howell put you up to this, I suppose,' Case said. He stared at her, awaiting an answer that never came.

Ella had expected anger, an explosion of rage after Case had spoken to Zebulon Becker down at the barn. Instead, the rancher seemed more saddened than angry.

She presented a dilemma, Case had admitted, one that was completely unexpected. Not knowing how much she knew, he could not send her back to the Howell cabin. Confining her on the ranch was problematic, too, should Howell or anyone else come out here. One more facet of this dilemma was the persistent rumor of bluecoat troopers on the march from the territorial capital to Denver.

'We have known one another for a long time, haven't we, Miss Campbell?'

he said. He studied her. 'Your betrayal is all the more painful for it.'

'In war,' Cahill said, 'spies are executed.'

'Yes, I know,' Case said.

Ella heard a serious intent resonate in his deep voice. Dizzying emotions surged through her. She met his gaze, but still held her silence.

'It would appear my choices are narrowed to two,' Case went on. 'Take you along as a prisoner. Or hang you.'

Jason made a sound. In a swift glance Ella saw his youthful face contorted, tears welling in his eyes. Jared, as stone-faced as his father, elbowed him.

Case paused again, then said: 'Well, perhaps your name will appear in a volume of history one day . . . 'Miss Ella Mae Campbell, the first prisoner of war in Colorado Territory'.'

★　★　★

Howell was joined by Jake Osborne, who assumed the rôle of second in command.

Osborne had some military experience, and suggested these men form the 1st Colorado Militia. A group identity would give them a greater sense of purpose, he confided to Howell, and encourage their fighting spirit.

Howell agreed to this. He knew the men were antsy. They had planned to ride out at midnight, but by the time they had secured equipment and food, and waited for latecomers, the hour was closer to three in the morning.

At Howell's command, then, they mounted and set out by starlight, only to be further delayed by five men too drunk to sit their saddles. Osborne sent them back when he discovered their condition. With the late start and delays, a hard ride brought eighteen of them to the crest of the rise overlooking the L-Bar-C well after dawn.

So much for the element of surprise, Howell thought, glassing the ranch buildings with the brass telescope loaned to him a long time ago by Bernard Cleeve. The corrals down there were empty, the barn door closed.

'See anything?' Osborne asked.

Howell shook his head. He raised his arm and swiftly brought it down. At this prearranged signal, the militiamen spurred their horses and swept into the grassy draw, guns at the ready.

Mallards fled with panicked splashes across the pond, and took wing. The men searched the house and outbuildings, quickly discovering the advantage of surprise was not needed. The L-Bar-C Ranch was manned by three cooks, none armed, none willing to talk. Ella Mae Campbell was not here.

Osborne questioned the cooks at gunpoint. Then he threatened them. All three refused to speak to him. He strode back to Howell.

'Hang one of them gents,' he advised in a voice loud enough to carry, 'and the other two, they'll tell us everything they ever knowed.'

Howell declined this Draconian measure. He shook his head again when several men offered to take the cooks out behind the woodshed. Others threatened to burn the ranch to the ground, taking the base of operations away from the enemy.

Howell silenced all of these threats. By his observation, the freight wagon and two buckboards were gone. So were saddle mounts and gear. He knew little of the strategies of warfare, no more than information gleaned from a haphazard reading of world history over the years — and most of that in praise of generals. Even so, he sensed more delays here would only give the enemy more time to prepare for a confrontation.

Howell and Osborne found the trail leading away from the ranch. The destination of the mounted Confederates was unknown, but day-old wagon wheel tracks and the prints of fifty-odd shod horses pointed the way.

'Water your mounts and get some rest,' Howell told the men of the 1st Colorado Militia. 'We've got a long, hard ride ahead of us.'

15

Ella coughed as she sat beside Jason on the bench seat of the buckboard. The seat was not wide, and they were close together. Dust sifted up from the hoofs of the team and from the column of horsemen ahead.

Ella wrapped a handkerchief over her nose and mouth, bandit-like, and breathed through that. Under her was a folded wool blanket, a poor cushion, but far better than none at all. The wagon had no springs on either the axles or the seat, and every pebble encountered by an iron-tired wheel sent shock waves reverberating through the seat, and through her. Worse, the uneven terrain rocked the wagon, turning her stomach as though she sat in a rowboat in high seas.

Ella cast sidelong glances at Jason. His face was boyish, his jaw beardless. She still thought of him as that scrawny kid fishing from the bank of the Mississippi River in the summer of '60. He had told anyone who would listen that he'd catch a whiskered catfish, one of those bottom-feeding lunkers big enough to supply meals for him and his father and brother or anyone else who happened by their campsite. Bernard Cleeve had teased him, saying a catfish that size would pull a skinny kid like him into the river and have him for supper. Jason had stood in mud past his bare ankles and cast a baited hook as far into the river as he could, reaching for deep water in his determination to prove Cleeve wrong.

It was a time of innocence and eagerness, Ella realized now, a time when every member of the wagon company was safe and guided by a single purpose, all of them eager for the challenges that lay ahead. It was a time when philosophical and religious differences were not at issue.

When Ella thought back, recalling the tangled and vivid events that had transpired since that day wagons and livestock were ferried across the great muddy river until this moment on the vast prairie, she did not weep. She rarely wept or dwelt on sorrows that had befallen her. For she knew other emigrants to the frontier had suffered mightily since leaving 'home.' A toddler playing in the shade under a wagon had been crushed by a wheel when the team had spooked and the wagon lurched; an experienced horseman had been thrown, dying instantly from a broken neck; on a new farm south of Denver ptomaine poisoning had claimed a family of eight, their bodies lying undiscovered for weeks. Ella knew the tragedies in her life were neither greater nor more profound than the parents of that little boy, or the young wife of that horseman, or the distant relatives of that entire family.

Perhaps, someday, she would weep again, but not this day. The crucible of life experiences had taught her to be strong in the present moment. She had learned to honor the past for what it was — her own unique history, a life she hoped others would know about one day. Why that was important to her, she did not know, but she felt it deeply.

Even though she was held under duress, Ella did not fear for her life. She knew little about Aaron Cahill, but she sensed Levi Case did not have the stomach for hanging a woman, spy or not. She expected to be confined for a time, and then released when this Confederate mission, whatever it was, had been completed. Then she would return to Denver.

She glanced at Jason again when he complained under his breath. Face pimpled, his voice still betrayed a child's manner. Unlike his brother, he was at the mercy of childish moods, an immaturity not yet outgrown to be forever left behind. The day was hot, he said, the ride tiresome, the dust choked him, and he wished he was riding horseback alongside his brother at the head of the column instead of back here with Ella in his custody.

His brother stood on the precipice

of manhood. But even though Jared emulated his father at every turn, even though his voice was deepening, and even though he had 'known' a woman named Christina as Ella had overheard him boast to the L-Bar-C riders, he was not yet a man. He acted the part. The more intense his performance, in Ella's estimation, the less convincing the rôle.

'Why do you keep looking at me?' Jason demanded as he held slack in the lines. He glowered at her when she did not immediately reply.

'I was just remembering.'

'Remembering what?'

'The Brethren Wagon Company,' she replied, 'gathering on the bank of the Mississippi River.'

'That was a long time ago,' he said irritably. After a pause he looked at her and asked: 'What about it?'

'I was trying to remember if you ever caught a big catfish out of that muddy water.'

Jason shook his head once, dismissing the subject. 'My father says I am not to

speak to you. You are a shit-eating traitor. That's what all the men say. I reckon
it's true. We trusted you, but you spied
on us.'

That hot day and two more like it
passed with rest stops at water holes.
Ella discovered these riders had previ-
ously found drainages and small springs,
and now traveled from one to another in
a twisting route across a seemingly dry
and barren plain. To what purpose or
destination, she did not know until the
next afternoon when the column halted
early.

They camped on a flat near a grass-
choked spring. Cahill donned his
Confederate officer's uniform and strut-
ted about, issuing orders. First, pickets
were stationed in pairs, muskets at the
ready. Every canteen and container was
filled from the bug-infested spring at the
edge of the campsite.

'If an attack comes,' Cahill said, 'the
victor will very likely be the one that
does not run out of water.'

Attack? Ella thought as she looked

around the barren plain. *From whom?*

Several men brought in firewood. They built a bonfire, the billowing smoke fragrant with the odor of sage. Most of the men were occupied with digging a series of slit trenches in the configuration of a V. From the camp, the V pointed toward distant mountains, giving the men a protected field of fire straight ahead as well to the left and right flanks.

They pitched two-man tents, and waited under a hot sun. Throughout the day, a number of men piled more fuel on the bonfire. Crackling and popping, flames leaped high, the fire raging all evening and late into the night. In the morning they built it up again with more sagebrush and dried roots.

A haze of smoke obscured the glow of the rising sun when a picket spotted a shadowy figure in the distance. A man on horseback approached them. He held the lead rope of a gray donkey.

Even though confined to the wagon at the rear of the column, Ella heard the man's profane shouts. She recognized the voice and vocabulary of Zebulon Becker.

'Don't shoot me! God damn it all, don't none of ye trigger-happy, gray-coat bastards shoot me! Whut's all that god-damn' smoke fer?'

'Perhaps you do not remember,' Cahill said. 'You told us to light a signal fire.'

Becker drew rein and dismounted. 'I never tol' ye to burn up the whole god-damned prairie, did I?'

The harsh words drifted to Ella's ears, along with an urgent question posed by Levi Case.

'Sir, where is this interpreter you promised to bring?'

'Don't worry yerself, Case. The 'breed I tol' you about, he's a-coming. He's a-bringing Bow Strings.'

'Bow Strings.'

'Warriors,' Becker replied. 'They know yer here. Cautious as wildcats, damned if they ain't. When the stinking bastards show, ye can palaver with 'em all ye want.' He dropped the reins. 'Here's yer saddle horse, Case. Me and Becky Sue, we'll hike outta here soon as you fork over my pay.'

'One thing at a time, Mister Becker,' Levi Case said. 'One thing at a time.'

Becker muttered a curse and strode away, tugging on Becky Sue's rope as he led the donkey to water.

Jason drifted away from the buckboard to join his father and brother. From a narrowing patch of shade cast by the wagon, Ella watched the men fashion a rope corral by the spring. Horses were confined at the water hole, each one hobbled as a precaution against a stampede should lightning flash or a windstorm blow up. These men had quickly learned saddle mounts were more than a convenience. In this region anyone caught afoot courted death from the elements or from savages.

Ella heard a shouted warning. With the others, she turned and peered to the west and north. In the first light of day she saw movement — riders mounted on spotted ponies had eased out of the foothills. When they drew closer, she counted eleven warriors. Bows and flint-tipped arrows in hand, they were led by Eagle Feather. A lone horseman moved up at his side. The war party halted. Each warrior studied the camp.

Ella watched the rider beside Eagle Feather. Young and lithe, black hair cropped short, he wore the garb of a white man.

'Seth,' she said aloud.

* * *

Riding stirrup to stirrup with Jake Osborne, Peter Howell set a fast pace — as fast as he dared. The churned trail leading across the rolling prairie hills was easy to follow. Water was plentiful. The Confederates would be slowed by two buckboard wagons and one freight outfit. At some point Howell knew the 1st Colorado Militia would close the distance. But when?

He did not have a way to estimate the time factor in this pursuit. Outgunned, he worried about bumping up against the Confederate force without warning. Or, as Osborne pointed out, they might scout their back trail and set up an ambush. With such worries sifting through his thoughts, Howell pressed on.

The men had been fired up to white heat by his abolitionist sermons. They looked to him for leadership. But with time to mull things over now, bravado cooled. Long, dusty hours in the saddle brought second thoughts and severe reconsiderations. One rider, a loyal church member named Orris Smith, simply turned his horse and rode back the way they had come without a word to anyone, ignoring the shouts ordering him to return to the line. Another, Ed Hargrove, complained of heat fatigue and dizziness, and hinted he would turn back, too. One other volunteer discovered he had brought a leaky canteen, and constantly begged for water from the others.

Tensions rising, Howell evoked the Golden Rule to settle the issue and try to maintain their cohesiveness. When the carping continued, Osborne cursed. He had heard enough, and abruptly hauled back on the reins as he turned in his saddle to face them.

'Ride to glory!' he said. 'Ride to glory, or slink home a coward. Ever' damned one of you. What's it gonna be?'

Howell eyed the big man. Osborne went on to address each volunteer by name, challenging them to stick or break off, with no more complaining. They stuck. In that moment Howell realized Jake Osborne was a natural leader, better qualified to ride at the head of this column than he was.

Howell thought about the leadership rôle that had been thrust upon him from here to the pulpit. The irony of it was not lost on him. He recalled the words of a pundit, the name long forgotten: 'History repeats itself, but never in a manner we expect.' The aphorism tied in with Howell's conviction that God works in ways mysterious to mortal man. One year ago he had ridden in hard pursuit of the captors of Ella Mae Campbell. One year ago he had been a follower, bone-deep scared as he had ridden a limping mule behind Earl Campbell and the rescue party. Now, one year later, another rescue party tracked the captors of Ella Mae Campbell. Howell rode at the head of this one.

From time to time he looked back. He saw bearded, stoic faces framed by dirty hat brims and sweat-crusted bandannas. Clouds of dust turned these men into a ghostly brigade.

Jake Osborne was not a man to turn tail, but the next day Howell learned second thoughts troubled him, too. He commented privately on the heat fatigue afflicting these men, adding his belief that this so-called militia was little more than a bunch of townsmen with guns. Their eagerness to punish slaveholding Rebs had carried them this far, but how much farther he did not know.

'We're chasin' fifty well-armed men,' Osborne said. 'A disciplined fightin' force can chew us up and spit out the bloody pieces without breaking a sweat.'

'I know.'

Osborne studied him. 'Preacher, if these men get the notion they're ridin' to their deaths, they'll run.'

'I know that, too.'

'What do you aim to do?'

'I'll tell you this evening,' he replied. 'All of you.'

At dusk Howell gathered the volunteers around his campfire. Braced for another hellfire sermon, they soon relaxed. The preacher did not raise his voice to evoke higher powers. He merely reached into his saddlebag and drew out a square of white fabric. It had come from Jane's sewing basket.

Howell showed the flag and confided the details of his plan. His goal was two-fold. Rather than engaging in a pitched battle with a superior force, he meant to confront Levi Case, gentleman to gentleman. For this purpose, he had brought a white flag. Under its truce, he meant to face Case and seek freedom for Ella Mae. As a gentleman, Case would either comply or demand a trial in a Confederate state. As a practical matter, he believed Case would free Ella Mae. That done, the 1st Colorado Militia would return to Denver where Howell planned to convey detailed information about the Confederates to the territorial governor.

'At that point,' Howell said, 'the U.S. Army will take over and complete the task of defeating the forces of evil.'

As though a great weight had been lifted, Osborne and the others heartily approved. One man stood, spat, and shouted a prediction that drew rousing cheers: 'One hundred strong, a company of Federals will whup fifty Rebs, sure as hell!'

'And you men of the First Colorado Militia,' Howell addressed the men again as his gaze scanned the fire-lit faces, 'will rightfully claim a share of God's glory in our victory.'

★ ★ ★

Ella's eyes were on Seth when he broke away from the war party. He urged the pinto up the slope of the hill, a nimble pony no doubt borrowed from the Cheyennes for this trek out of the mountains. Zebulon Becker must have convinced him to accompany warriors to this site, Ella thought, and then translate during a meeting, unusual as it was. She started to edge closer, halting when she became aware of a stench.

Becker came up from the rope corral and slipped behind her. Now he grabbed her arm. He pulled her to the far side of the wagon, his foul odor enveloping her. She struggled, but his other hand grasped her neck as he yanked her closer to him. That hand squeezed.

'I heard these god-damned Rebs talking about hanging ye, girlie. Feel the noose tighten, do ye now?'

'Let . . . let go!'

'Girlie, I'll walk ye outta this god-damned Reb camp safe and sound,' he whispered, 'if ye show yer handsome gratitude to me later . . . .'

Ella jerked away and faced him. 'I'd rather hang.'

'Maybe ye will,' he said, reaching for her again, 'if I'm not here to save yer god-damned bacon.'

She side-stepped him. 'Remember what happened last time you grabbed me . . . .'

Becker cursed her.

Ella moved away from the buckboard. She tried to overhear the words Seth was exchanging with Cahill and Case. Behind her, Becker hissed again.

'I done tol' them Rebs not to give guns to the Bow Strings,' he said. 'Ye gotta swap goods with 'em. Ye gotta get respect from the stinking bastards. Seth, he'll tell 'em.'

Ella turned to him. 'Free? The guns are . . . are a gift?'

The shaggy head nodded in disgust. 'A new musket's worth five buffalo robes. Five! Them stinking savages, they won't show no respect without a swap. Fair fer fair.' He repeated: 'Seth knows. He'll tell 'em.'

'I . . . I don't understand,' Ella said. 'Why are Mister Case and Colonel Cahill giving guns away?'

'They done boiled up a plan to arm the Cheyennes,' Becker replied. 'A plan all the way from Richmond, Virginia, I hear tell.'

'Plan? What plan?'

'Give the stinking bastards a few guns,' Becker said, 'and Bow Strings kin raid farms and ranches through the whole god-damned territory. Folks'll be screaming fer protection. If bluecoats march out here, see, that gives the Rebs back East better odds. Don't it now?'

Ella stared at the shaggy trader in disbelief. At once, though, she knew this vile man had no reason to invent such a scheme.

Becker went on: 'Colonel Cahill, he says when the South wins the war, tribal lands will be returned to the Cheyennes. Says a treaty's signed and sealed by Jeff Davis hisself. All the Bow Strings gotta do is fire them muskets at farmers and cowhands, steal some horses, attack a town or two. Settlers will be screaming bloody murder. Git my meanin', girlie?'

Ella turned away. She understood all too well. The Southerners would use the warriors to open a second front. She had heard her father talk about guerrilla warfare. In the American Revolution poorly equipped patriots had defeated rows of redcoats by attacking from hidden positions in the woods or behind stone fences before fleeing. Unconventional as it was, that type of combat made sense in the West — and explained why Levi Case had quietly brought so many riders to the L-Bar-C. If farmers, ranchers, or miners were frightened by Indian attacks, Confederates under the command of Cahill could move in and secure property and mines fancied by the South.

She left Becker there and strode closer to Case and Cahill. With their backs to her, her presence went unnoticed by most of them. Only Seth faced her. His gaze found her. She shook her head when his eye lingered on her. The moment passed, and Seth turned his attention back to the man in uniform, Aaron Cahill.

'Eagle Feather and the warriors see long knives,' Seth said. 'Your knives come out of the earth like the spines of a steel cactus. That is what they say.'

'Bayonets,' Cahill corrected him. 'Tell them we've merely taken a defensive posture. They have nothing to fear from us.'

Seth shook his head. 'The warriors see your men hiding. They see guns pointed at them. They will ride no closer.'

'We won't shoot first,' Cahill insisted. 'You have my word. Go tell them.'

'Your word is not enough,' Seth said.

Cahill stiffened. 'You listen to me, you half-breed savage. My word is my bond. Don't you forget it, or I'll have you flogged.'

'No matter what I tell them,' Seth said, 'the warriors will come no closer.'

Levi Case stepped toward Seth. 'Don't you understand? One round from a rifled musket will knock a man off his feet at two hundred yards. Tell those savages that if we had intended to kill them, we'd have done it by now.'

'If you challenge them,' Seth said, 'they will fight.'

'Just tell them,' Cahill added, 'that we have come here to give them muskets. Tell them we'll equip them and teach them how to use and maintain these weapons. They can defeat their enemies with these guns. Tell them that.'

'We also brought brass kettles,' Case said, 'along with skinning knives, awls, and calico cloth for their women folk. Go on now. Tell them.'

Seth turned his pony, his single-eyed gaze sweeping past Ella. He rode to the warriors clustered there. They sat their ponies and spoke to each other for a long time, each man having his say. Then the warriors withdrew. Seth came back alone.

'What's going on?' Cahill demanded.

'They will speak to their old man chiefs about this,' Seth said.

'What does that mean?' Cahill asked.

'They will seek advice from tribal elders,' Seth answered, 'before they make a decision about talking to you.'

In frustration Cahill yanked off his plumed hat and slapped it against his leg. 'How long will this rigmarole take?'

'Not long,' Seth replied. 'The chiefs have traveled from their encampment by the blue lake to a place called Shadow Valley, a three-day ride from here.'

'Three days!' Cahill protested. 'How long will they leave us sitting here . . . a week? Two weeks? Longer?'

'How much time is needed to make a decision?' Seth asked rhetorically. He added: 'It has to be reasoned out.'

'Reason,' Cahill scoffed. 'What do these savages know about reason? How can anyone do business with them?'

Ella saw Seth pause before replying. 'They have the same doubts about you.'

Both Cahill and Case looked at Seth in surprise. Cahill demanded: 'What do you mean by that?'

'Think about what they know,' Seth replied, 'and you will know what I mean.'

'We're not here to play parlor games,' Case said. 'Tell us precisely what you are driving at.'

'First, you sent a message through Zebulon Becker,' Seth said. 'The men of the tribe do not trust him. Then Becker came for me. I gave them your message. They do not trust you.'

'Why?' Cahill demanded.

'White men have murdered Cheyennes and Arapahoes,' Seth replied. 'Eagle Feather's family was slain by buffalo hunters. Now the Bow Strings see your men hiding with long knives and guns aimed at them.'

Neither Case nor Cahill had a ready response. Case broke the silence.

'Well, I must confess,' he said, 'we have not thought about it in those terms. We merely bivouacked in accordance with standard military procedures.'

Aaron Cahill ran a hand through his fine hair, and clapped his hat on his head. 'All right. Catch up with them. Tell them we await their decision. Their prompt decision.'

Seth gazed at him as though peering over a divide, a distance so great that neither side clearly saw the other. He started to speak, but then turned the spotted pony.

Levi Case added: 'Be certain you deliver our most important message to those savages.'

Seth halted and looked back.

'President Jefferson Davis has signed a treaty promising to return all lands to them,' Case said. 'That treaty will be law after the Cheyennes help us win the war. Make certain you tell them that.'

Ella saw Seth lift a hand in acknowledgement. He urged the pony into a trot and rode after the departing warriors.

She returned to the buckboard. She looked around, relieved that the trader, Becker, was neither seen nor heard — or smelled. Through the morning she followed a patch of shade around the vehicle. She drank from a canteen. When she refilled it at the spring, she noticed Becker's donkey was not among the horses.

At noon Jason brought food to her. She asked about Zebulon Becker. He was gone, Jason told her. The Indian trader had left camp with Becky Sue in tow, one hundred dollars richer.

16

Howell used the brass telescope to scan the terrain ahead. He looked for flights of small birds common to the prairie lands, or a whisp of smoke from a campfire. He saw neither, no obvious signs of riders other than dry earth churned by two hundred shod hoofs and six sets of wagon wheels. The trail was as clear here as it had been since they departed the ranch, but now horse droppings were fresher. More than ever, Howell sensed they were closing the distance. He slowed the pace to a walk, peering ahead as they crested each swell in a stilled sea.

Movement came in the form of a man on foot. Howell brought the telescope to bear on the figure leading a mouse-gray donkey. Lowering the instrument, he grimaced as though encountering another link in a chain of bad luck.

'Who is it?' Osborne asked, reining up beside Howell.

'Becker,' he replied. He turned to the men behind them and raised his voice. 'Some of you may know Zebulon Becker. He's an Indian trader, lately tied in with Levi Case, somehow.'

'Keep your weapons handy,' Osborne added.

The riders reined up. Dismounting, they drew muskets from saddle scabbards and checked the loads. Some walked around, stretching sore leg muscles while waiting for the lone man. Howell and Osborne sat their horses. The terrain was flat. Zebulon Becker was clearly alone.

'What the hell ye doin' out here in the middle of nowhere?' Becker demanded of them when he drew closer.

'And good day to you, sir,' Howell said. He pushed his broad-brimmed hat up on his forehead.

Becker squinted. 'Preacher? It's you, ain't it?'

'It's me.'

'What the hell ye doin' out here? Bringin' God to a God-forsaken place?'

Howell waited while Becker finished laughing at his own joke. 'Where are the Confederates?'

'Over yonder,' Becker replied, jerking his thumb back the way he had come.

'How far?'

He shrugged.

'How long have you been walking since you left their camp?'

'Dunno,' he replied. 'I've been out here long enough fer my sweat to sour up, I kin tell ye that.'

At that moment Becky Sue pulled away, fighting the rope until Becker yanked on it, holding her fast.

Observing the donkey, Osborne muttered: 'Not even that ass can stand your stink.'

'Climb down offen yer horse!' Becker said. He reached for his knife. 'Damn ye, climb down and face me like a man!'

With half a grin, Osborne shook his head.

'Ye ain't no kinda man then, are ye?' Becker taunted. 'Yer some kinda girlie wearin' a man's pants.'

'Fact is,' Osborne said, 'I can't stand to get any closer to your stink, either.'

Amid more curses, Howell nudged his horse between them. He raised his voice and addressed Becker. 'Is Miss Campbell with the Confederates?'

Becker glowered past the horse at Osborne before turning his gaze to Howell. He nodded once.

'Is she all right?' Howell asked.

'Last I seen of her, she was.'

'She's in danger?'

'There's talk of stringing her up fer a spy.'

'Levi Case is not that kind of man,' Howell said.

Becker shrugged. 'Reckon you know him better than I do.'

'What's the Reb camp look like?' Howell asked.

'Two squads on a stretch of flat land,' Becker said. 'They's dug in near water. Ready fer war, damned if they ain't.'

Becker glanced at the townsmen standing by their horses. 'If ye aim to attack them Rebs head on, ever' damned one of ye will die under a hot sun. I kin tell ye that fer a certain fact.'

'We're not here to fight,' Howell said. 'We've come for Miss Campbell.'

Becker squinted. 'Jest how do ye aim to tell that to Cahill before the shootin' starts?'

Howell hesitated. 'Looks like we could use your help as a go-between, Becker.'

Becker considered that. 'Fer my fee of one hunnert dollars, I reckon I could carry yer message.' He added: 'Fifty dollars right now, and fifty more after I do your job fer ye.'

Anger flashed through Howell. 'You can help us save lives for no fee at all.'

Becker shook his head, eyeing Howell and Osborne. 'To tell ye the unvarnished truth, ye got a way of raising my goddamned dander. Both of ye. My fee jest climbed to two hunnert dollars . . . .'

'Your fee,' Jake Osborne interrupted, 'just got throwed out.'

'Huh?'

'No dollars from us,' Osborne said, 'and no busted-out teeth for you.'

Becker snarled like a cornered coyote, his hand again darting to the bone handle of his sheathed knife. 'Aiming to get yerself hurt now, ain't ye, girlie pants?'

Osborne drew his pistol, thumbing back the hammer with a well-oiled click. 'Mister, leave that knife where it is, or I'll be obliged to take it off your dead body.'

Becker smirked at him, his hand grasping the handle now. 'Maybe ye can pull that trigger and git a ball into me, but I know I kin bury my blade in yer god-damned gut. Ye'll bleed like a stuck pig. Ye won't die fer a few days, but ever' damned minute ye'll be thinking of me, wishin' ye'd backed off. That's the god-damned truth, girlie pants.'

Now Osborne cursed him, lifting the gun.

'Jake,' Howell said. 'Jake, let it go. We don't need him.'

Osborne hesitated, jaw clenching, when Becker again taunted him. He eased the hammer down and holstered his handgun.

'Truth is, ye don't wanna fire off a

gun this close to the Rebs,' Becker said. 'That's the god-damned truth, ain't it? Well, ain't it?'

Turning to the trader, Howell said: 'I suggest you go on about your business, Becker . . . now.'

'Good god-damned riddance to ye,' he said, yanking on the rope. 'There's plenty more I could tell ye about them Rebs, but ye won't get a word outta me.'

This time the long-eared donkey set her hoofs. Becker yanked on the rope. She did not budge. Becker swore. He fed out the slack in the rope, drew it back, and lashed her with the knotted end. The donkey hopped once and farted twice, and set off trotting down the trail with Becker high-stepping behind her.

Howell watched him jog away in boots held together with strands of twisted wire, each scuffing step raising dust.

'That man walks the face of the earth like the devil hisself, don't he?' Osborne said.

Howell nodded. 'I do believe he matches Satan stride for stride.'

On the flat occupied by the Confederates, prairie heat bore down on man and
beast for one scorching day after another,
sunup to sundown. With no afternoon
storms and no clouds to break the heat,
high temperatures radiated from a brassy
sun in a blue sky like steam from a fired
boiler.

Ella had brought her quilt, the one
that her grandmother had made for her
a long time ago, a long way from here.
Now she spread it under the buckboard
and took shelter in the shade there. At
night this patch of hard, rocky ground
was her bed. Levi Case and his sons
had backed the buckboard farther away
from the men and their corralled horses,
leaving her alone with Jared and Jason
alternating in guard duty. As much to
guard the prisoner, she knew, their purpose was to remind the men that this
area was off limits to them.

In the night Ella heard two voices, one
giggling, the other giddy with a barely

controlled undertone of laughter. She picked up enough to know it was Jared who stood alongside Jason, two lanky shadows in near-darkness. Laughing out loud, Jared boasted to Jason of his conquest.

'That preacher's girl wanted it, Jase, I'm telling you. Christina wanted it bad, and I gave it to her good! You should have seen that bucking she-devil!' His description of the act performed behind a stack of lumber was interrupted when Ella raised up on an elbow and in a loud voice threatened to tell their father.

Jared cursed her, calling her 'nothing but a damned spy.' He quickly moved away from the buckboard, leaving Jason behind to complete his shift.

The next night Ella was disturbed by soft sounds near her. Her eyes opened. Reality and dreams overlapped in her mind as she woke up. The sounds of someone moving on the ground close to her brought back memories . . . memories of awakening under her family's Conestoga wagon in the darkness before dawn of that awful day. Her kidnapping and captivity by Cheyennes still lived in her daydreams and nightmares, but these sounds were real. In the next moment someone touched her.

'Ella.'

She half turned and raised up. The whispering voice was familiar. She saw the shadowy figure in the starlight, and her heart surged as she recognized him.

'Ella,' Seth whispered again.

She pushed the quilted blanket aside and crawled out under the far side of the buckboard. Seth reached for her. Grasping his hand, she came out and leaned close, alerting him to the presence of a sentry. She looked around. Neither Jason nor Jared stood near the wagon.

'Asleep,' Seth whispered. 'All asleep. Hurry.'

She spotted the rounded forms of two prone figures on the ground by the front wheel of the buckboard. Jared and Jason were asleep, their muskets leaning against the hub of a spoked wheel.

Ella pulled on her shoes. She quickly

gathered her belongings in a carpetbag, and grabbed two corked canteens. She moved away from the wagon.

By the light of stars, Seth led her out of camp, one quiet step at a time. Ella feared the pounding of her heart and the roar of her breathing would awaken the camp like a drum-and-bugle call. No sounds of alarm erupted behind them, though, and from the spring they moved away swiftly, leaving behind fifty men sleeping in two-man tents. Then corralled horses whinnied.

Ella halted behind Seth. They knelt and remained still as stones for several minutes. Finally the restless Morgans calmed. No alarm was raised by a sentry.

Sentry. Ella looked around. By starlight she saw no sentries — not one. She understood then what Seth had meant when he had said 'all asleep.' The heat, she realized, had battered all of them into exhaustion, and at night, while the whole camp slept, the sentries dozed, too.

Making their way through clumps

of sagebrush and around pear cactus, Ella followed Seth into a shallow gully. Deepening, it wound past a low hill. Well beyond the Confederate camp, she saw a pair of spotted ponies in the starlight. Both were tied to sagebrush.

Seth untied the pintos and tossed a pair of reins to her. They led the ponies farther away from the camp. Ella drew a deep breath. She relaxed a bit. Behind them lay the silence of the night.

A safe distance away, they mounted and left the ravine. Riding bareback across the open prairie, Ella held on to her carpetbag with one hand and a fistful of mane with the other. Their pace would be slow, Seth had told her, to save the ponies' strength. If Cahill sent a squad of Confederates at daybreak, the two of them would have to make a run.

An hour before sunup, they halted at another spring, a pool of water reflecting the stars like a black mirror. They knelt and filled the canteens. Then they rested while the ponies drank and grazed on sparse grass growing along the bank of the spring.

She tried to peer into his dark eye by the dim light. 'You brought my father's watch to my room.'

It was not a question, but clearly a statement in search of an answer. Unable to read his expression, she waited for him to speak. When he did not, she asked: 'Why didn't you stay at the ranch . . . stay long enough for me to thank you?'

'I am not welcome in the white man's world,' he said, 'and I would not like to bring trouble to you.'

'But how did you know where to find me?'

'When Becker said I would be paid to translate,' he replied, 'he told me you were there. I rode to the ranch on a pony borrowed from Eagle Feather.' He paused. 'I saw you at the window by lamplight. I waited, out of sight from white men. Next day a windstorm swirled out of the sky like an angry spirit, and you rushed out the back door to the clothesline. I went in through the front, and left your room through the window.' He added:

'When I went back to the blue lake, I led the Bow Strings to the graycoat soldiers. They burned a signal fire. We found them waiting. Their guns were aimed at us, their long knives ready to cut us.' Again he paused. 'I carried the messages of the white men to the Bow Strings.'

'What will the warriors do?' she asked.

He shrugged. 'The old man chiefs will decide.'

After sunup her question was closer to an answer, when Seth abruptly reined up. Halting, he pointed to a plume of dust sifting into the sky. They both observed it for a time. The dust was stirred by a column of riders.

Ella soon recognized Peter Howell. He rode beside Jake Osborne at the head of the line. With one look at Seth, she knew what she must do now.

She dismounted and handed the reins of the pony to him. He gazed down at her, and smiled.

'Thank you,' she said. She reached up to grasp his hand. 'Thank you.'

She stepped back. With a last look at

her, Seth turned the ponies and rode away.

Even though the men of the 1st Colorado Militia had ample water, they were clearly suffering in the relentless heat. Shoulders sagging this morning, their gazes were downcast as though their heads had grown heavy, as thick and dull as melons. With no scouts sent ahead, they did not see Ella on the trail until they came upon her, a young woman standing alone in the empty prairie, carpetbag at her feet, bonnet shading her eyes.

* * *

History repeats, Howell once again recalled the aphorism, but never in a manner we expect. He stared at Ella Mae Campbell. He stared as though seeing a mirage on the Great Plains. He stared at an apparition that could not be real . . . .

Yet the sight before him seemed real. Ella Mae stood on the trail ahead — alone, unmoving, watchful. He slowly lifted his hat in greeting, still wondering if this was an illusion, a waking dream seen by him alone.

In those moments Howell remembered a sunny Sunday morning one year ago when the bleating shrieks of Millicent Campbell had interrupted the singing of hymns. His congregation was silenced one voice at a time as their heads turned, one by one, to find the source of those strange noises.

Howell had looked, too. He saw the gaunt woman pointing to a figure across the South Platte River. Now that same figure stood before him like the mythical Columbia come to life, her long dress much soiled, her head covered with a dusty, sweat-rimmed sunbonnet. She raised her hand in answer to his silent greeting.

'I'll be damned,' Osborne whispered now. He quickly added: 'Pardon my blasphemy, Preacher.'

'Perhaps we all should be,' Howell murmured. Calling her name then, he spurred his horse ahead.

History, he learned from Ella Mae, had repeated itself when the one-eyed youth, Seth, had once again freed her from captivity and delivered her to safety. With the militia drawing into sight, Seth had left her on the trail and headed back to his hunting ground in Shadow Valley. From there, he would carry messages from the old man chiefs to Levi Case and Aaron Cahill.

Now, from Ella's account, Howell and the men of the 1st Colorado Militia learned the details of the Confederates' camp and their weaponry, as well as a scheme of arming Cheyenne warriors to wage guerrilla warfare in the West. At last Howell fully understood the motives of Levi Case and Aaron Cahill. And now with corroboration from Ella Mae, he no longer doubted the accuracy of Becker's terse assessment. Every man in this rag-tag militia knew if they drew close to that fortified position without a truce, they would be gunned down with a few well-placed volleys.

'Gentlemen, we have achieved our

goal,' Howell announced to the gathered townsmen. He examined their faces as a minister examines his congregation. He saw that his statement was met with quiet relief. The townsmen stole glances at one another, but none spoke. Howell went on: 'We shall let the U.S. Army take over from here. We can only pray troopers will be dispatched before it is too late.'

While no one gave voice to a larger truth, straightened postures and quick smiles among the men of the 1st Colorado Militia told it. They were not merely relieved to be turning back, they were elated. Not a man among them, though, would reveal even a hint of cowardice by a spoken word or an unguarded expression. Stone-faced, they quietly turned their horses, Denver-bound.

Two hours past noon of that day, Osborne spotted a dust cloud smudging the hot sky. The big man stood in his stirrups, hat brim shading his eyes.

'Somebody's on the trail, Preacher,' he said. 'A big bunch, heading this way.'

Fear surged through Howell in a cold wave. He raised his arm. At that signal, the townsmen halted. With Ella Mae riding behind him, Howell swung his leg over the saddle horn and slid to the ground. He helped her down, and quickly opened his saddlebags. He feared another Confederate force had been sent to aid Cahill's command, with the Colorado Militia caught in the middle. Yanking the brass telescope out of a saddlebag, he pulled the instrument open and steadied it across his saddle. He peered through the lenses. Relief swept over him.

'Gentlemen,' Howell said, straightening up, 'our prayers have been answered.'

'Prayers?' Osborne asked. 'Or nightmares?'

Howell passed the telescope to him. Osborne looked through it, grinned, and uttered a single word: 'Bluecoats.'

Advance scouts soon drew into view. Half a dozen mounted troopers preceded a company of dust-laden infantry. Howell observed them. Even from a distance, he saw clean-shaven soldiers. Ramrod straight, they were well-equipped and battle-ready. The company marched under a swallow-tailed guidon, a small flag bearing an abbreviated version of the Stars and Stripes.

Other than Fourth of July parades back in Delaware, Howell had never seen soldiers in formation before. Even from this distance, one hundred troopers with muskets over their shoulders and full packs on their backs made a formidable sight, an unstoppable force crossing the low, cactus-studded hills of the prairie. What came after them was more impressive yet.

The company was followed by five Army supply wagons, horsed-drawn water tankers, and two twelve-pound cannons, each with limbers bearing caissons. An infantry major and a captain of artillery rode ahead of the column on horseback while two mounted lieutenants flanked the troopers. A burly troop sergeant and four corporals marched on foot with their men.

The ranking officer spurred his horse. He galloped ahead, obviously not surprised to see the armed townsmen on this stretch of prairie.

'I am Major Jonathan Winslow, United States Army,' he said, reining up. 'Which one of you is Howell?'

'I am,' Howell said.

Winslow dismounted. He was lean and severe in his expression, his dark blue uniform powdered with dust. The officer's flinty gaze swept past Ella to the bedraggled townsmen, and then he stood aside for his infantry to pass.

After the scouts came the main line of march. Howell watched the soldiers troop by in route step, eyes sweeping left and right as they gazed with some curiosity at the gathered townsmen. The leather soles and hard rubber heels of two hundred boots pounding dry earth made a dull rhythm — as dull and ponderous as a dirge, Howell thought. In a crescendo, the heavy vehicles rumbled past with the two bronze cannons and artillery crews.

'I encountered a civilian on the trail who informed me of your presence,' Winslow said after the last two-wheeled limber rolled by. 'A trader by the name of Becker. Know him?'

'All too well,' Howell said.

Winslow cast a slight smile at him. 'The man gave contradictory answers to my questions. I was reluctant to turn him loose and hand him an opportunity to warn the enemy. So I placed him under arrest and sent him back to Denver with an escort.' Winslow paused. 'This man, Becker, apparently believes you plan to confront a Confederate force.'

'We are out-numbered and out-gunned,' Howell said. 'Our purpose was to locate the Confederates. I wanted to free Miss Campbell from their custody, and report to the territorial governor.'

'I see,' Winslow said. 'And did you locate them?'

'In a manner.'

'What manner?'

Howell gestured to Ella Mae and introduced her. 'Miss Campbell spent several days with the Rebels as their prisoner, Major. She managed to escape last night, and just hours ago reported to me. She knows where the Confederates are dug in.'

Winslow turned to her. He removed his hat, and stepped closer. He questioned her, listening intently while she described the size of the armed force, the terrain, and the master plan Levi Case and Aaron Cahill claimed came from Jefferson Davis himself.

'As far as I am concerned,' Winslow said with a confirming glance at his captain, 'Mister Case and this jack-colonel, Cahill, have committed treason.'

The artillery officer nodded. 'Should they survive our cannonade, they'll hang.'

Howell noticed Ella Mae staring at the two officers, and saw her wince at the captain's statement. Howell was not surprised by it, but the casual tone of their voices sent a cold stab through him, too. In the next moment he was aware of Winslow speaking to him.

'Your name is familiar to me.'

Howell turned to the major. 'Sir?'

'I am aware of urgent requests for assistance by you and other civilians in Denver,' Winslow explained. 'I can tell you that we have new intelligence reports indicating a Rebel force will make a push before winter sets in. Denver is to be torched, burned to the ground. The Confederates' next objective is to capture gold mines . . . a prize offering a source of much needed bullion.' He added: 'Our purpose here is to stop them. Stop them dead in their tracks.'

Caught up in the moment, Osborne said: 'I'll ride with you, Major. Reckon I can help you and your men . . . .'

Winslow turned swiftly and interrupted him. 'Sir, I know you mean well. However, by authority of the federal government, I am ordering you to return to Denver, all of you, with the exception of Mister Howell and Miss Campbell.'

Osborne started to protest.

'Sir,' Winslow said, cutting him off, 'this is not a subject for debate. I expect to have my hands full by dawn tomorrow, or sooner, with no time to nursemaid Sunday soldiers.'

Osborne said: 'But I got somethin' to settle with Mister Levi Case . . . .'

Howell moved between them, facing Osborne. 'Jake.'

Osborne avoided his gaze.

'Jake,' Howell repeated. 'Remember . . . vengeance is not yours for the taking.'

'I remember,' Osborne said dully. He looked at him. 'But there's something you gotta know. Your preaching don't take my pain away. Not for one minute.'

Major Winslow turned and moved to his horse. With practiced ease, he thrust a boot into the stirrup, and swung up into the saddle. From horseback he addressed Osborne and the other townsmen.

'Gentlemen,' he said, 'I am determined to turn back this Rebel force. If the Confederates gain a foothold out here in the territory, more will come. Now, you men return to Denver. Prepare to defend your town. That is my order, and I expect you to do your duty and carry it out.'

Winslow swung his horse around and faced Ella Mae Campbell. 'Now I have a request to ask of you, miss.'

'Request?' she asked.

'Double up, and ride behind Mister Howell,' Winslow said. 'Guide us to that ravine . . . the dry wash you mentioned near the enemy position. We will take up firing positions tonight. You will be held out of harm's way, both of you.'

Howell looked at Ella Mae, awaiting her reply.

'You are asking a terrible thing,' she murmured with a glance at both men.

'Miss,' Winslow said, 'I am asking for your loyalty to the Union.'

She offered no answer to his implied question.

'Will you assist me,' he demanded, 'or by your refusal will you aid your kidnappers?'

She looked him in the eye now. 'I will take you as far as the ravine.'

Winslow turned to Howell, clearly

pleased. 'Out here in the West, we rarely have the opportunity to engage a massed force. My men relish an opportunity to put their training into practice. Our cannons throw twelve-pound explosive shells for a distance of a thousand yards. Both artillery pieces will be rolled into place tonight while my infantry belly-crawls, flanking the enemy. When we shell their position at dawn, the Rebels will either die in those slit trenches, or be cut down in fusillades of musket fire if they attempt to break out.'

Ella felt tears leap to her eyes. 'But . . . but can't they surrender?'

'Surrender,' the major repeated in disgust. 'When the Rebel guns are silent, that will mark the moment of surrender.'

Ella cast a doubtful look at him. 'But you are giving them no choice.'

'Tell me, Miss Campbell,' the major said, 'if the situation were reversed, do you believe for one moment the enemy would show us any mercy?'

Without waiting for her reply, Winslow started to ride away. Then he abruptly drew rein. He turned in the saddle, giving her a second, measured look.

'Make no mistake, miss,' he said. 'This is war, not some schoolyard game. We mean to send a message from the frontier, a message even Jefferson Davis cannot ignore.'

17

Ella did not intend to weep. Sitting on the horse behind Peter Howell, she was neither prepared for a surge of raw emotions, nor for the depth of her concern for Levi Case and his sons. Head bowed now, she quietly wept, hoping Howell and the others would not see her tears or quaking shoulders.

She had noticed Winslow's mystified expression when he had demanded affirmation of her loyalty to the Union. She knew that he thought it was bizarre for her to feel sympathy toward her captors, that she must be half mad.

By all rights, she should have despised Levi Case and his sons. On one level of her thinking, she did. She knew Case to be a harsh taskmaster; she knew Jared was hostile and mean at times; she knew Jason was a whiner, soft, apologetic, and nearly the opposite of his father and brother.

But on another, deeper level, she

remembered her long and intertwined relationship with all of them, a relationship beginning with a scrawny kid she had seen fishing from the eastern bank of the Big Muddy. Other poignant memories crowded into her mind, and with them came more tears. No matter what Winslow thought of her, she simply could not set aside her feelings for them.

When she had agreed to serve as guide, she had held out an ill-defined hope that she could convince Winslow to allow her to speak to Levi Case, a wild notion that she could affect a truce of some sort. Yet at once she knew such a request would not be granted. The major was right — perhaps more than he knew. Cahill was not a man to surrender. He would never give up to Yankees or agree to any truce with his sworn enemies. Now, as they drew closer to the ravine that had been an escape route for her and Seth, she knew events were closing rapidly, the outcome well beyond her control.

From a distance the land ahead was no more than a dark crease in the prairie. Ella looked over Howell's shoulder, seeing the ancient riverbed, eroded and dry in the vast prairie. This ravine was a vivid reminder. Many Bears had taken her to one like it.

'The Confederate camp is about half a mile from here,' Ella said, and saw Winslow immediately rein to a halt. 'Their horses are held in a rope corral,' she added, 'near a spring.'

At dusk the ravine was scouted and, by nightfall, declared to be suitable passage for the artillery pieces and caissons. The cannon were moved closer to the flat expanse of prairie occupied by the Confederates, both weapons manhandled as they were quietly eased into firing positions. After dark, troopers were sent in. Leaving packs behind, along with gear that could clank or rattle and give them away, the infantrymen belly-crawled forward, flanking the enemy position. Anyone fleeing the cannonade would be caught in a crossfire.

At midnight Ella overheard a lieutenant report to Winslow. The two men spoke in low voices. The junior officer had seen a signal fire burning bright in the Confederate position, and he had crawled in close before backing off, undetected.

'The Rebs don't know we're here,' the lieutenant said. 'They act like they're on a Sunday picnic back home.'

'Damned fools,' Winslow said with a note of compassion in his voice. 'Poor damned fools.'

* * *

In the dim starlight Howell watched a lean figure approaching the supply wagons and water tankers. Major Winslow emerged from the night shadows after a last word to his officers. He moved close to Howell, and spoke in a low tone of voice.

'You and Miss Campbell stay back here with the wagons,' he said, 'and you will be out of harm's way. Don't wander. My men are out there, fingers tight on the triggers.' He added: 'I offer my thanks to you and Miss Campbell for your service. As soon as this thing's over, I will provide an escort to Denver for you both.'

Howell watched him stride away, saber in hand now. He had settled in for the long, sleepless hours until dawn, or believed he had, when a soft, muffled cry reached him. He found Ella Mae wrapped in her quilt where she sat on the ground beside a supply wagon. Her hands covered her face.

'Ella Mae, are you all right?' he asked, kneeling beside her.

'Yes,' she whispered.

'You're crying,' he said, and heard her draw a ragged breath.

He felt helpless in the presence of a woman's tears. Sitting beside her, he pulled off his hat and leaned back against the wagon wheel.

For several moments Howell looked up at the stars, gazing at the countless pinpoints of light in a black sky. During his career as a minister he had often been asked one heartfelt question: if there is a

God in His heaven, then why . . . ?

As a young preacher quick to spout glib answers to life's great conundrums, he had believed in a God of revenge and swift punishment. Howell's task was to uncover errant behavior, his voice loudly naming sin as the source of earthly misery. These discussions inevitably led to blame, accusations, condemnations, and more misery.

Now as a man hip-deep in middle age, Howell had been changed by the events that had transpired since leaving home. In the West he accepted life as it came to him, no longer issuing threats of eternal damnation. He urged his congregation to practice forgiveness in their lives, to believe in the power of spiritual compassion, and to remember God works in ways mysterious to mortal man.

Howell looked at Ella Mae in the near-darkness. She possessed her father's bravery. In her, he had never seen anguish born of self-pity or blame. She had suffered, he well knew, but she had been strengthened by ordeals that would have broken a weaker woman. Her tears were genuine, hard-earned.

'I do believe,' Howell whispered at last, 'that my daughter's been on a crying jag ever since you left us to work for Levi. Given everything that has happened since then, I wish you had stayed with us, I truly do.' He paused. 'I hope you will come back to live with us.'

Ella did not reply.

'At least consider it,' he said.

Howell put his arm around her shoulders. He felt her head rest against him. He did not think he would sleep, but fatigue caught up with him. His eyes closed, opening suddenly with the first explosion.

The great, shuddering roar of a field cannon brought him awake in an instant. He felt the ground shake and heard a distant *whump*. One exploding shell was quickly followed by another as the gunners found the range. The air filled with an acrid smell of powder smoke. Cannon fired twice a minute in a full barrage now, each shell exploding with that sound so

soft and deadly — *whump* . . . *whump* . . .
whump.

Howell became aware of a tightness in his arm. Ella Mae had grasped his sleeve. She held on as though drowning. He put his hand over hers. He had the sense they were drowning — not in water, but drowning in sound and the sheer force of the explosions. The roar of one cannon alternated with the other, both guns firing repeatedly, and the cannonade seemed to go on forever. In truth, it was over in a matter of minutes.

Howell got to his feet. The first light of day shone through a pall of powder smoke. The eastern horizon turned pale pink in those first moments of daybreak when shadows in the ravine still held the darkness of the night.

Moments after the big guns fell silent, he heard the crackle of musket fire. Then those weapons were quiet, too. A grimace came to Howell's beard-stubbled face. He felt sick to his stomach. He had read enough about warfare to know what came next — thrusting bayonets in a *coup de grâce* charge of infantrymen.

The silence after battle, Howell discovered, was like no other. As loud and furious as the bombardment had been in those minutes of great din followed by staccato gunfire, the quietude now was as deep and seemingly as endless. Deathly quiet was the expression that came to mind as he stepped away from the wagon.

Howell looked around. The only way to find out who had survived was to see for himself. Permission to move closer to the field of battle would never be granted to him by Winslow. He knew that. Seeing no one to stop him, he made his decision and edged toward the ravine.

'Stay here,' he said to Ella Mae over his shoulder, and started off through the dry wash in long strides, unaware that she had scrambled to her feet.

★ ★ ★

Preacher Howell lunged ahead of her, somewhere. She had lost sight of him after he broke into a run in the bottom of the ravine. Now she rushed past the cannon and limbers. Both gun crews were gone, probably to inspect the field of battle for themselves.

The first sounds to reach her were the squeals of wounded horses, innocent brutes injured by shrapnel and bullets. She drew closer to the camp. Another hundred feet, and she came in sight of the rope corral. Most of the L-Bar-C Morgans were down. Some kicked as they tried in vain to stand, others banged their bloodied heads against the earth in their agony.

She halted. A bluecoat soldier was ahead. He was a young man alone, dazed and dirty as he leaned on his musket for support.

Ella slowed. She climbed out of the ravine. Whether the soldier was a sentry or not, he made no effort to stop her. He seemed to stare past her, or through her, with no recognition appearing in his eyes. She moved by him, and stopped as though struck by a fist. The sight before her was the reason for that soldier's empty stare.

Strewn with corpses, the remnants of two-man tents, and uprooted cacti and rabbitbrush, the earth was churned as though great plows had turned the soil in a mad, criss-crossing path. Shell craters pocked this expanse of churned prairie, a piece of ground no larger than a schoolyard.

Ella moved past the L-Bar-C buckboard wagons and the lone freight outfit. All three vehicles were heavily damaged with broken wheels and burned canvas covers. The wagon Ella had slept under lay on its side like a ship blown out of the water, smoldering as it sent a haze of smoke drifting into the morning sky. She saw bluecoat soldiers wandering among the dead, heads bowed, every man silent.

Disbelief washed over her, a dizzying sensation that clashed with reality. She could neither believe the sight before her, nor deny it. Splashes of blood, chunks of flesh, jagged white bones — all were strewn across this killing field with human legs, arms, heads, torsos. The gore was spread through slit trenches and in the craters created by exploding cannon shells. Of the fifty, few bodies were whole. Most were blown into pieces, large and small, bloodied all.

Her gaze distracted, she nearly tripped over a corpse at her feet. She stood over the remains of a battered body bearing a familiar face. It was the young man with a waxed mustache who had confronted her in the carriage with Peter Howell and Christina on the ranch road, the one she had seen smartly present arms to Cahill at the guarded door of the barn. Now the young man lay sprawled on his back, jacket blood-soaked from shrapnel buried in his chest like hammered spikes, lifeless eyes staring skyward.

Ella lifted her gaze, wondering if prisoners had been taken, and where they were being held. She looked around, knowing that notion was a false hope. The battle had unfolded as Winslow had predicted. In all likelihood the barrage of cannon fire had killed most of these men in the first few minutes. Those who had attempted to flee were cut down by musket fire. The only wounds suffered by bluecoats, Ella overheard the troop sergeant report to a lieutenant, were cactus spines picked up while belly crawling in the darkness to reach their firing positions.

Ella heard a sob. Turning, she saw Peter Howell on his knees. Anguished cries wracked him. She moved closer and looked over his shoulder. On the ground the silver-bearded Levi Case lay dead, a slender corpse in his arms. In death, the father clutched the body of his youngest son, as though still protecting Jason from the horror. A dozen yards away Jared was sprawled on the ground, too, musket clenched in his lifeless hands, one leg twisted awkwardly underneath him, the other blown off.

Ella moved away. Among the mangled bodies, she recognized the remains of Aaron Cahill by his uniform. Hatless, his skull was broken open like a dropped jug, his fine hair blood-caked.

Ella was startled by pistol shots. Howell jumped, too, quivering as though cold. Ella turned. She saw mortally wounded horses being put down by soldiers.

Ella moved to the preacher's side. Bending down, she grasped his arm, and helped him stand.

* * *

'Company! March!'

Major Winslow's company of infantry did not tarry. Leaving the dead where they had fallen, the column headed back to Denver with the confiscated materiel and the remaining Morgan horses. Ella had thought she was numbed to the sight of carnage until the foot soldiers marched over the rise in the prairie overlooking the L-Bar-C Ranch — or what was left of the ranch.

First, she stared. Then came tears, as though this scene of destruction triggered pent-up grief. Where the ranch house, barn, and outbuildings had once stood were now piles of burned timbers and heaps of gray ashes, blackened stove pipe chimneys and charred bed frames.

When the infantrymen drew close, mallards quacked and swam madly for cover in the cat-tails of the pond. Across the way, a long-eared jack rabbit bounded away, and redwing blackbirds took flight. No other living creatures were in sight. Even the vegetable garden had been purposely trampled by shod hoofs.

Howell exclaimed over this scene of devastation. While soldiers rested and horses drank at the pond, Ella overheard a conversation between him and Winslow.

'On our march through here,' the major said, 'we detained and questioned three ranch cooks. They were uncooperative. I sent them to Denver under guard. We picked up the Confederates' trail, and followed it.'

Winslow had determined the ranch to be a Rebel outpost. That had been his justification for destroying it.

In Denver, details of the battle became

known to the citizenry only after blue-coat soldiers returned from the killing ground and described it. The Confederate position, so daunting to the 1st Colorado Militia, had been merely a target for Winslow's artillery. In the major's view, this 'battle' was scarcely more than a training exercise with live fire.

Cahill's blood-caked gray uniform had been pulled from his body at the site, the half burned Confederate flag confiscated. To underscore a Union victory, Winslow ordered them exhibited in Denver. The uniform was draped over a stick scarecrow and placed in front of Cahill's saloon, the flag tossed into the dirt.

Noted for laying their eggs in the nests of other birds, cowbirds were common among herds of cattle. In this way, Cahill's deadfall of logs and dried mud did not stay empty for long. Zebulon Becker placed the Stars and Stripes over the door, and took the place as his own. The Confederate artifacts disappeared, and the former Indian trader became a purveyor of spirits and beers, pig's feet and pickles, two-cent cigars and nickel chaw.

In the aftermath of that first and last battle in the territory between Yankees and Rebels, many Southerners cashed out and left the territory for the long trek home. Their departures were not acts of surrender or an acknowledgement of defeat, but rather an eagerness to join the battle in regiments raised by their home states. The war had started there, folks said, and that was where it would end.

Christina wept when she learned of the violent deaths of Levi Case and his sons. Ella did not relate the details of the battle and gore to her. Neither she nor the Howells celebrated. More than ever, she recalled her father's words about warfare. He had been right. If joy and triumph and glory came with victory, she found none amid the death and carnage she had witnessed.

* * *

Soon after his return to Denver, Howell was taken aside by Jake Osborne. The man had picked up foul rumors circulating through town. These tales concerned Ella Mae Campbell. While she did not occupy one of the cribs by the river, it was commonly believed that poor Ella had turned to whoring. Added to her well-known sins of the flesh, now she was a traitor. According to cooks who had worked on the L-Bar-C Ranch, Ella had been well paid to work as a servant girl — too well paid for mere domestic labor.

'Men are sayin',' Osborne said, 'that she was nothin' but a brood mare to any stud in the bunkhouse who wanted a turn with her.'

She had traveled with the Confederates, as rumor had it, joining in their efforts to arm the bloodthirsty Cheyenne warriors and throw them against unsuspecting settlers. Worse, she then betrayed her benefactors by leading bluecoat troops in a surprise attack against the Confederates.

No matter which side the rumor-mongers favored, North or South, all of them agreed traitors were lower than vermin. With more news of tremendous battles being waged back East, war fever intensified in Denver. Outrage flared anew, inspiring death threats. Traitors are hanged, men in Denver said, and someone surely ought to bring Ella Mae Campbell to justice.

Howell listened in disbelief to these yarns Osborne had heard. A thread of factual information gave them a measure of credibility — no more than a measure, Howell thought, for new rumors contradicted old ones. What about her supposed hatred of savages? Why would she help arm them to kill settlers?

Ella Mae, as far as Howell knew, had not yet caught wind of the tales. Most of her time was spent at the Howell cabin and garden, or on the crest of the bluff where she tended the graves. She kept to herself, he noticed, sometimes sewing with Christina.

Howell often thought back to Earl

Campbell's words in July of 1860: 'If I don't make it back, Peter, I want you to look out for Millie.' Howell had done that to the best of his ability. He felt the same obligation to Ella Mae. He was determined to counter the lies. Sunday mornings, his booming voice raged against the evil of falsehood.

'Give mouth or ear to cruel rumor,' he said, 'and you perform the work of Satan! Will you join the allies of evil, my brethren, or devote your words and deeds to the forces of good?'

Howell endured catcalls while carrying his message into saloons and livery barns. A saloon man with short-cropped hair and a fresh shave threatened him with a length of stove wood, and drove him out of the place. Lunging outside, Howell tripped over a log and fell. Aside from the embarrassment, he suffered a parting stream of curses from the proprietor, standing in the doorway.

'Git out, god damn ye! Git out and stay out of my place!'

Only then did Howell realize his tormentor was Zebulon Becker.

Howell picked himself up. He looked down. The cottonwood log he had tripped over was pocked. Two names were carved into the soft wood — **Jared** and **Jason**.

Like wind-driven brush fires that cannot be stomped out by one pair of boots, persistent rumors about Ella flared. Each one took on a life of its own. In the end, rumors merely shifted, swirling into the imaginary smoke-filled winds of new and more scandalous tales. For Peter Howell, it was a painful lesson, learned again, about human nature.

Ella had done nothing to deserve such vile treatment. Howell fell into despair. For the first time in his life, he faced a crisis of his faith. The age-old question — If God is in His heaven, then why . . . ? — now gripped him.

While injustice unfolded before his eyes, vivid dreams visited him nightly. Most carried images of Levi Case in death, a father clutching his youngest son with the dismembered corpse of his eldest sprawled nearby. The sight and smell and sound of the battlefield that day had entered his dreams, memories constantly relived.

Howell became fearful of sleep. He dreaded the night. Jane and Christina helped him pray for release from this curse. He meditated, awaiting a message, a sign from above. It came from ground level.

'Peter,' Jane said, 'members of our congregation scorn falsehood. Most do not believe the lies told about Ella Mae.'

She was right, of course. As a family, they had discussed this before — and with Christina, too, after she had heard rumors about her friend. Jane was merely reminding him of the truth. But he also knew seeds of doubt could be planted in pure hearts. His calling was to join the battle against evil, to wage the good fight to save souls. For eternity.

'Peter,' Jane said, 'I have been thinking about this.'

Their conversation was interrupted when the door opened. Christina stepped into the cabin. Making sure she was alone for the moment, Jane motioned for her to close the door and come in.

'We were just talking about Ella Mae,' Jane said.

'What about her?'

'All those mean-spirited lies circulating about her,' she replied. 'Does she know about any of them?'

Christina shook her head.

'We must tell her.'

Alarmed, Christina blurted: 'No!'

Jane repeated firmly: 'Chrissy, we should be the ones to tell her.'

'But that would be cruel!'

'Think of the cruelty,' Jane said, 'when Ella Mae finally learns of these hateful rumors from someone else . . . and realizes we have already heard them.'

Howell waited no longer. After supper in the cabin the four of them sat at a table with a smoky tallow candle burning in a holder. Howell drew a deep breath. He turned to Ella Mae. After a long moment he spoke to her, sparing no details. He was surprised by her stillness, awed by her courage. She was genuinely unmoved by the slanderous tales and fearless of threats against her life.

'I am avoided in town like a leper,' Ella said. 'I suspected it had something to do with my captivity by Cheyennes. People seem to think the Indians cast a spell and made me into an immoral woman. Why do people believe such tales?'

Howell shrugged. 'Why are people attracted to evil?'

Ella thought about that. 'All any of us can do is find the right path in life.'

Howell stared at her. So did Jane and Christina. The three of them fell silent in the presence of a fundamental truth. Ella went on to thank the Howells for their love and concern for her well-being. Then she made an announcement.

'This is a good time to tell you.'

Jane asked: 'Tell us what?'

'I have some money,' Ella said. 'I guess you could say I have chosen my path. I've decided to leave Denver.'

In that moment a great weight lifted from Peter Howell's spirit. His mind raced ahead. Stagecoaches now ran regular routes between Denver and North Platte, and, from there, passenger train service was available. He assumed Ella Mae would travel by these conveyances on a journey back East.

'I have made clothes suitable for travel by horseback,' Ella went on. 'Now I will buy a horse and saddle.'

Howell said: 'Surely you do not intend to cross the prairie alone . . . .'

'No,' Ella interrupted. 'I intend to ride into the mountains.' She added: 'Alone.'

'Mountains,' Howell repeated.

'To a place called Shadow Valley,' she said. 'I know a route to get there, and I know I will be safe when I arrive.'

There was further discussion over the next several days, but Howell could not dissuade her, and quit trying. Ella knew her own mind, and her mind was made up. He had to agree with her statement that she well knew of the dangers of such a trek. She would succeed, he realized, where he had failed.

For the first time in weeks peace

came to Peter Howell. He slept soundly through dreamless nights. He thought of Levi Case in a different way. Case himself had set in motion events leading to his death and the deaths of Jared and Jason.

Howell remembered the man's lies. Case had first lied about his intentions of forming a militia to free Ella Mae from the savages. A year later he had deceived Howell and everyone else in Denver about his plans for waging war in the territory. He had kidnapped Ella Mae, and in the end, Howell thought now, underestimating her had been his greatest mistake. She understood politics and current events. With wisdom beyond her years, she sensed the consequences of warfare on this prairie better than the shortsighted people who were so quick to fight.

'Your father would be proud of you,' Howell said before she left. 'So would your mother.'

With the help of a liveryman who belonged to the First Brethren Church,

Ella picked out a chocolate brown mare, a small but sturdy saddle mount accustomed to traversing mountain trails. Then, in a last walk on the sandy bank of the river, Christina took her arm and held it tightly.

'Elly Mae, I will always be grateful to you,' Christina said. She added in a whisper: 'You know why.'

Ella smiled at her.

'You are a loyal friend,' Christina went on. 'You kept my dark secret. You protected me from cruel rumors. And you saved my parents from pain and humiliation.'

She hesitated before adding: 'You saved me from hating myself, too.'

'We've been close for a long time,' Ella said. 'We always will be.'

'I'll miss you so much,' Christina said, her voice quavering. 'Elly Mae, I must tell you. I'm worried. I don't know what's going to happen to you.'

'I'll be all right.'

'Promise you will come back for visits,' Christina said. 'I know you keep your promises.'

'Promise,' Ella whispered, and they embraced.

Afterword

I found my way to Shadow Valley, Ella Mae Campbell wrote, **and Seth Carter found me. We married under the rule of common law. Four angels came to us. Two daughters and two sons. My grandchildren live in an era when some white people boast of a direct lineage to the Indians. They claim a tribal branch in family trees, a branch offering supernatural powers. It was not always so.**

* * *

Shivering, Pastor Sue Tracy pulled a shawl over her shoulders. The day was like any other New Year's Day in Denver — cold, clear, sunny — yet vastly different. This one was the first day of January in a new millennium.

2000. A subject for her next sermon, the number still seemed strange and unwieldy to her.

She shivered again. This time of year sunlight filtered in through the stained glass windows of her office in the First Brethren Church. Century-old leaded glass spread elongated geometric patterns of soft colors across the hardwood floor, colors that brightened and faded with the angle of the sun through the day.

On the desk before her were the diaries of Ella Mae Campbell and an unfinished memoir written by the church founder, Peter Howell. To this volume, notes had been added by Jane Howell after Peter's death in the summer of 1892. A legendary figure, until now Sue Tracy had found only flowery passages recounting the man's achievements, all of them written much later by church historians. Howell Hall in the church had been named for him. As a minister, Sue had read, he was noted for concluding his sermons with the familiar phrase: 'For eternity.'

Sue knew Howell's congregation had built a small stone and plank church on the bluff overlooking an open stretch of prairie and the river. Earth-movers had sculpted and re-shaped the landscape, but the church was still there. Expanded and remodeled many times over the decades, including re-burial of the graves from the Pioneer Cemetery, now the First Brethren Church was surrounded by high-rise buildings, belted by streets crowded with cars, trucks, buses.

She found herself coming back to the diaries. In Ella Mae, she felt the presence of a strong voice from the past, a voice commemorated by the congregation of 1900. The life led by Ella Mae Campbell, and the fact that she had not only survived but had lived a long and productive life, amazed Sue.

Something else caught her attention. Late in his life, Howell had made a bizarre claim. Like the Son of God, he said, he had once been lost in the wilderness. After forty days he saw the face of Satan.

Passages in the memoir clarified that claim. Howell saw Zebulon Becker. He saw the man who saved his life by providing food and guiding him out of the mountains. He saw the man who took pleasure in cursing him. He saw the man he had endeavored to forgive for the remainder of his days on earth.

Shadow Valley never produced a single flake of placer gold or an ounce of silver, and was thus spared the onslaught that befell other Rocky Mountain valleys and water-bearing gulches in the second half of the 19th Century. The place remained untouched through all the years Ella Mae and Seth nurtured their four angels. Even the People of the Blue Lake kept their summer ground until later in that century. All too soon, though, Cheyennes and Arapahoes, as well as Utes, had been rounded up by the Army and sent off to reservations. Confined to narrow regions and fed government surplus food — much of it teeming with maggots — the People were never allowed to return to their summer hunting ground on the shore of the lake.

According to Ella Mae Campbell, the old man chiefs of the tribe had smoked around an evening campfire in Shadow Valley during that hot July of 1861. Passing the pipe while silently watching the flames had meant their hearts and minds were one. The oldest among them had spoken first, then the other men had given voice to their concerns.

Ella Mae had listened while Seth translated. Having seen for themselves the aftermath of a battle between blue-coats and graycoats, they had been baffled by the utter destructiveness of such warfare. The abandonment of their dead had been a source of scorn among these tribal leaders. The time would come, they all had agreed, when great armies of murderous white men would set upon one another in a violent battle. All would die. Then the tribes would be free to walk their lands again.

Sue gazed at the diaries and memoir on her desk. Her eyes moved to a gold pocket watch that had been placed in the Colorado Fuel & Iron box one hundred years ago. She picked it up and wound the stem, smiling to see that it still ran.

She pressed the release, and read the inscription again, a wedding gift from Millicent to her beloved husband, Earl, so long ago.

When Sue had first lifted this time-piece from the strongbox, she had thought: *Oh, if only it could talk. What stories it could tell . . . .*

Now as the heavy gold watch was warmed by her hand, ticking as though alive, she realized it had spoken to her, to everyone.

We do hope that you have enjoyed reading this large print book.

Did you know that all of our titles are available for purchase?

We publish a wide range of high quality large print books including:
Romances, Mysteries, Classics
General Fiction
Non Fiction and Westerns

Special interest titles available in large print are:
The Little Oxford Dictionary
Music Book, Song Book
Hymn Book, Service Book

Also available from us courtesy of Oxford University Press:
Young Readers' Dictionary
(large print edition)
Young Readers' Thesaurus
(large print edition)

For further information or a free brochure, please contact us at:
Ulverscroft Large Print Books Ltd.,
The Green, Bradgate Road, Anstey,
Leicester, LE7 7FU, England.
Tel: (00 44) **0116 236 4325**
Fax: (00 44) **0116 234 0205**

Other titles in the
Linford Western Library:

SIX-GUN BOSS

Clay Randall

The three big cattle outfits of New Orlando are being bled dry by rustlers. Pat Reagan, range detective for the Texas Panhandle Stockmen's Association, is assigned to work undercover as a ranch hand for George Albert of the Box-A, and bring the thieves to justice. But the only law around there is that of the six-gun and the noose — and when the glamorous daughter of George makes a play for Pat, he's heading into deep trouble . . .